A deadly bomb attack at the courthouse has left two people dead, and all of the evidence so far points to Alyssa Bristol as the perpetrator. She was placed under arrest, and that was arguably the *least* distressing part of her day.

Extricated from police custody by her friend Abby, both women have become fugitives, and are being pursued by two relentless police detectives, who have enough evidence to charge Alyssa with domestic terrorism and two counts of murder.

There is also the matter of an alarmingly violent assailant, seemingly determined to leave a trail of destruction in their rampage across the city.

Alyssa is on the run and has no time to clear her name, so it will be up to her friends and family to solve the mystery before it's too late.

A brief recap of how we got here...

The Target:

Alyssa Bristol found out the hard way her parents (Malcolm Mercer and Mary Bristol) were spies, when a group of their enemies, led by mercenary Henry Castle, abducted her. She was rescued and protected by Abby Lunay, a criminal-for-hire, through Abby's employer, Marcus Coltrane.

Abby was born with a rare neurological condition, where her brain is naturally in a locked state, leaving her largely comatose. Hard alcohol allows her brain to function, but her consumption levels are causing damage to her body; her estimated time to live ranges from five months to five years.

The Estate:

What was initially described by Alyssa's Great-Uncle Sal Zanetti as a simple house-sitting job turned into a haunted nightmare, as Alyssa and Abby had their hands full with an angry ghost and three difficult Zanetti heirs. The ghost was terrifying, yet still easier to deal with than the family.

In an effort to ween Abby off the alcohol, Alyssa began working on a root-based herbal medicine for her. Although the results have been mixed, there has also been some progress.

Abby moved in with Alyssa's family, as she had been living in a small storage room above Marcus' bar.

The Suspect:

It is now August, and Alyssa has turned eighteen, graduated from high school, and is working part-time at the same law firm her Uncle Sal works at. She works in the mailroom, focusing mostly on copy jobs, document preparation, and sorting projects based on their due date.

Abby is still doing 'errands' for Marcus. These 'errands' are most often of an illegal nature, which is why they've earned the quotation marks. She has, however, noticed an improvement in her health, as Alyssa's medicine is finally working better than the alcohol had been.

Which brings us to the horrific and murderous events about to unfold today...

August 16

12:08 p.m.

The sound of the explosion lasted only a fraction of a second, but the blast itself immediately killed the two the men nearby. The resulting fire inside of the courtroom was relatively small, but it nevertheless caused a large-scale reaction. Within seconds, alarms were blaring, people were shouting, and a quick-thinking security guard began spraying the flames with a nearby fire extinguisher, creating a thick, eerie, grey fog inside the room.

Outside the courtroom door, Alyssa Bristol stood confused, while people ran past her, going in and out of the room. The courthouse went into full lockdown protocol, and it would be nearly two hours before Alyssa would be allowed to leave so she could head back to the law firm of Dryden-Halbeck, where she was working.

Alyssa had delivered more than a box of documents to the courthouse. She had also delivered the lethal explosives.

August 17

1:06 p.m.

The boardroom was a long, rectangular shape, and was dimly lit by an array of round lights which were inset in the ceiling. There were three mahogany-coloured conference tables, arranged end to end, with sixteen tan-coloured leather chairs around them.

When Alyssa Bristol entered the room, there were only two people inside, both of whom were wearing suits and staring at her. She assumed they were the two police detectives she had been asked to speak with in order to give them her statement.

One of the men was leaning against the wall. He was a younger person, likely late twenties or early thirties, and he seemed to have a natural scowl on his face. He had close-cropped black hair and a two-day growth of stubble on his tanned face.

The other man was seated in front of the leaning fellow. He was older, with thinning hair, salt-and-pepper beard, and a forehead highlighted with creases. He had reading glasses perched upon the bottom of his nose.

"Hello." The seated detective stood up and flashed a warm smile. "Are you Alyssa Bristol?"

"Yes."

"Please, have a seat and be comfortable." He waved his hand in the direction of one of the chairs. "I'm Detective Richard Newberg, and that's Detective Neil Browne."

Alyssa sat down. "It's nice to meet you, sir."

"My father was sir. There's no need to be formal here, so you can call me *detective* if you'd like. Now, just sit back and relax." Newberg sat back down, while Browne continued to stand and lean. Newberg picked up his pen and tapped it against his pad of yellow paper. "This is just an informal little chat to get your statement in the hopes we can better understand what took place yesterday. I realize this may be difficult for you, as it just happened yesterday, but we want to catch whoever did this, so we need you to simply do the best you can, okay?" He flashed a reassuring smile. "We've already taken the statements of the rest of the staff members on our list, and I've compiled quite a lot of helpful notes. Now it's your turn, so I'm hoping you'll help me add to those notes."

"Yes, of course." Alyssa had some difficulty getting comfortable, so she fidgeted in the chair. Yesterday's events were still fresh in her mind, and she had been trembling for most of the day. "The firm encouraged all of us to come in, provide our statements, and cooperate with you to the best of our abilities."

"I appreciate your helpful attitude, so thank you." Newberg cleared his throat. "Now, being curious, I do a little research on each person before I interview them, so I can get to know them a bit quicker. That way, we don't waste so much of your time with small talk, and we can get to the larger, more pressing matters. While I was looking you up, I couldn't help but notice that you've had a very busy year, haven't you?"

Alyssa exhaled sharply. "Yes, it's been a year unlike any other in my life, that's for sure. And I don't mean that in a good way."

"I can only imagine how you must feel after everything that's happened to you." Newberg looked at some scribbled notes he'd made on a separate page. "Kidnapped and chased this past spring, and then a month ago, there were some pretty wild ghost stories coming out of Washington State, which I understand involved you as well. And now this terrible and horrifying bombing of the courthouse. You've been through a lot, so you have my sympathy."

"Thank you."

"It's a lot for a person to deal with, especially a young person such as yourself." Newberg made some fresh notes on his notepad. "Have you attended any sort of trauma counseling?"

"Yes." Despite the cool temperature in the room, Alyssa could feel the prickly sensation of perspiration forming on her brow. "I've had several weekly sessions with a therapist over the past four months. I was at the point where I was considering checking in once every four weeks, but after what happened at the courthouse yesterday, I might keep it at weekly for a while longer."

"That's good." Newberg continued to write. "Not enough people take their mental health treatments seriously, so it's commendable that you're looking after yourself."

"Thank you." Alyssa fanned herself with her hand. "The firm sent a message to everyone saying they'd pay for whatever counselling anyone needed because of what happened yesterday."

"Nice." Newberg looked up from his notes. "Listen, before we get into the tragedy at the courthouse, may I ask you a few things about the unfortunate events you experienced this past April?"

"Sure, what did you want to know?"

"Your abduction last spring coincided with the busiest week for local first responders in nearly a decade. My counterpart in the Burnaby RCMP said they seized a van, allegedly owned by your abductors, which was loaded with assault weapons, military hardware, and all kinds of tactical gear. Then the van was seized from them by the federal government later that same week, with no explanation given. Close to the same time, here in Vancouver, a house exploded and burned to the ground. Security systems all over the metro area were hacked into and compromised, and guess what? The feds took over both of those investigations as well. One minute I'm working the case, the next minute four spooks from CSIS walk in and take everything I have on it and then drive away." Newberg shook his head. "It's not every day someone from the federal spy agency pulls a police case file right out of my hands, but that's exactly what happened. All of these bizarre and sometimes violent events seem to be connected to you, as your name keeps popping up in the middle of every one of them. That can't be coincidental, so we need to ask you a particularly big question."

"Yes," Detective Browne finally spoke. "We're curious about why the federal government is so interested in you."

Newberg leaned forward in his chair and nodded. "We're *really* curious."

Alyssa wrung her hands, then shrugged. "I'm sorry, but you'd have to ask them about that."

"That sounded like a non-answer to me." Newberg turned to face Browne. "Did that sound like a non-answer to you as well?"

"It really did sound like a non-answer." Browne narrowed his eyes as he studied Alyssa's face. "The last time the feds took over one of our investigations, it was tied to an imminent terror attack on the city. Can you at least tell me if there is a threat of some kind which is going to completely ruin my day?"

"I can definitely tell you that all of the people who were trying to abduct me are in a federal prison somewhere in the United States." She looked from one detective to the other. "I am not aware of any active threats against the city or anywhere else. Beyond that, though, I honestly don't know."

"Okay." Browne thought about her words for a moment. "That's something, anyway. Now, let's talk about the incident at the courthouse yesterday."

"Yes," Newberg sat ready with his pen and paper. "Please tell us in your own words what happened."

Alyssa took a deep breath and let it out slowly. "I dropped off the box of documents to Mr. Richardt, and then I went out into the hallway. A couple of seconds later, the explosion happened. Sorry, but I'm not sure exactly which parts you want to know more about."

"Then allow me to assist you, if you don't mind." Newberg resumed tapping his pen against the notepad. "Was the client, Mr. Zanikker, with Mr. Richardt when you went into the room?"

"Yes, they were sitting side-by-side at one of the tables located at the front of the courtroom."

"Then you were the last person to see them alive, weren't you?"

"I hadn't thought about it like that." Alyssa grimaced. "What a horrible thought. Yes, I guess that's true, now that you mention it."

"Let's go back to the beginning."

"To when I dropped the documents off?"

"No, back to the *very* beginning," Newberg twirled his pen with his fingers. "I want you to go back to when you first saw the box which you would later bring to the courthouse."

"Sure, uh… they keep the file boxes in the mailroom. They're flat, die-cut, and you just fold them into a box whenever you need one. I made up a box and set it on the counter beside the copier near the door."

"So, you made up the box yourself and set it on the counter," he said as he wrote. "Don't the mailroom staff do that kind of thing for you?"

"Until a month ago, I worked in the mailroom, so I could make one up just as quickly myself." Alyssa shrugged. "I didn't want to bother them to make one box when I could easily do it."

Newberg nodded and continued writing. "And then?"

"Ashley, the mailroom girl, is still new, and she was busy with an urgent copy job, so I did my own copying at the second copier. She cries when she gets stressed, which is often, and I didn't want to deal with that. The documents were needed for the afternoon portion of the trial, so we were in a time crunch. It was therefore practical for me to quickly do the job myself. While the copier was making copies, I'd be binding the completed pages and then I'd place the bound documents inside the box. Is this the information you're looking for?"

"Yes, it is, and this is very helpful." Newberg didn't look up from the notepad as he continued writing. "So, once you were done with all the documents, what then?"

"I counted the fourteen documents to make sure they were all there. Then I closed the lid, taped up the box, put it on a dolly, left the building, and delivered them to the courthouse."

Newberg finished writing, set his pen down, and then locked eyes with Alyssa. "Let's talk about some of those steps in more detail for a moment."

"Sure."

"Let's start from the point where you finished putting the box together, and then set it down on the counter. Was it out of your sight at any point?"

Alyssa shook her head. "Not while I was copying, no, but when I was binding the documents, yes. The binding machine requires me to turn my back, because when I'm standing at the copier, it's on the counter behind me."

Newberg picked up his pen and made another note. "Okay, so when you placed the final document inside the box, did you see anything other than documents inside of it?"

"No, there were fourteen bound documents inside the box, and nothing else." Alyssa's throat felt dry, and she could feel her fingers starting to tremble. "Like I told you, I re-counted them when I was finished, to make sure everything was there."

"Right, so at that point, you said you then taped up the box and put it onto a dolly." Newberg looked at his notes and nodded. "I've got a pretty clear picture about that part, so let's move forward from there. Did the box leave your sight at any point after that?"

Alyssa shook her head. "No."

"How can you be so certain?"

"Because I didn't leave any events out of what I told you earlier." Alyssa used her unsteady fingers to count off her next points. "I taped it up, put it on the dolly, wheeled it into an elevator, went down to the lobby, out the door, along West Georgia Street, then turned right and went down Hornby Street to the courthouse. I went straight to their courtroom, and then dropped the box off. As soon as I did that, I wheeled the dolly back out into the hallway, where I was going to begin the trip back to the office until… well, until the blast happened. The box was with me continuously from the mailroom to the courtroom."

Newberg made more notes. "So, to summarize, you were the last person to see the contents of the box before it was sealed."

Alyssa glared at him. "Yes, but I'm not sure I like the way you said that."

"And why is that?"

"Because you've now made a point of stating I was the last person to see inside the box *and* that I was the last person to see the victims alive." She stood up, eyes wide. "Wait, am I being accused of something?"

"No, we're just getting some details to add context to your statement, that's all." Browne narrowed his eyes. "Why? Is there something we should be accusing you of?"

"No, there isn't." Alyssa made her way to the credenza along the side wall. She poured herself a glass of water, spilling some due to the increased shakiness of her hands. "Is your theory that the bomb was inside the box?"

"It *used to* be my theory," Browne said, "but it's since been established as a fact, thanks to some quick analysis on the part of our forensics team. They've confirmed there were plastic explosives inside the box you delivered."

Alyssa took a drink, then set the glass down on the table. "Then there must be some mistake, because that's not possible."

"Uh huh," Newberg tapped his pen on the pad. "You're saying it's not possible because you didn't see any explosives inside of the box before you sealed it, correct?"

"Yes, that's exactly correct." Alyssa sat down and tapped the tip of her index finger on the boardroom table. "There were fourteen documents inside the box, and no explosives. None. Zero."

"Let's take a moment to recap what you and I have established in the past few minutes." Newberg picked up his notepad and began to read. "You personally made up the box, even though it wasn't your job. You personally prepared each document for the box, even though that wasn't your job either. You filled the box, you double-checked the contents, and then you sealed the box, delivered it, and you insisted to us that it didn't leave your sight at any point."

"Yes, but…"

"Do you know what else we've established?" Newberg glanced at Alyssa. "That you were just far enough away to be completely safe from the blast."

"I could have been killed."

Newberg threw his hands into the air and let them fall back to the table. "And yet you were lucky enough to emerge from yet another incident without a scratch. You've been impossibly lucky these past few months, haven't you?"

Alyssa's mouth hung agape for a moment. "I've had *terrible* luck lately, are you kidding me?"

"You just walked away unscathed from a bomb blast which killed two other people, so I'd hardly refer to that as having terrible luck." Newberg's voice grew increasingly louder as he went on. "And the courtroom tragedy is only the latest violent incident you've emerged unscathed from. Abductions, explosions, shoot-outs, fires, and now a bomb blast, all happening this year, I might add, and yet here you sit, without a single scratch. How do you *not* view yourself as the luckiest person on the continent?"

Alyssa's father, Malcolm, had always told her to be careful of what she shared with the police, and his words began echoing in her mind. She was confident a simple statement would be easy to provide, but now that she was seeing how her words were being used against her... she was sweating. Detective Newberg noticed, and pressed on.

"Miss Bristol, I need for you to tell me all about the four-leaf clovers you must be having for breakfast each morning, so I can better understand how all of this is even possible."

Alyssa rubbed her eyes. "I can't explain how I've survived everything, but I can tell you that not all scratches and scars are visible."

Newberg gave a slight nod and his voice calmed. "That's a fair point, but tell me how *you* think an explosive device got inside the box."

"I don't know." Alyssa slouched in the chair. "Like I said, I wasn't able to see the box the entire time I was preparing the documents. My back was turned while I was binding them."

"The mailroom supervisor, Sylvana Reyes…" Newberg flipped through some of his pages. "Here it is. She told me it takes around ninety seconds to bind a document. Would you agree with that assessment?"

"That's about right, yes."

"Okay, so then let me ask you this." Newberg thought for a moment before continuing. "How likely is it that someone knew *exactly* when you'd turn your back, so they could dash into the mailroom, remove all the documents from the box, place an explosive device inside it, place the documents back, and then leave without you seeing them, and all of that happening inside of only a ninety-second window?"

"It's probably unlikely."

"I'd agree, though I would have used the word *extremely* instead of *probably*." Newberg leaned forward. "Based on what you and everyone else has told us, you were the only person with both the means and opportunity to place an explosive device inside the box."

"But why would I hurt anyone?" Alyssa's voice cracked. "I have no reason to want either of the victims dead."

"Relax, Miss Bristol, I completely agree with you." He reached for the nearby box of tissues and slid it toward her. "You appear to have no motive whatsoever to kill either of the two victims. However, I do know the client made over seven-hundred enemies. I wonder how long it's going to take my team to see if one or more of those people are tied to you or your parents in some way?"

"My parents?" Alyssa sniffed, took a tissue, and then blew her nose. "What do they have to do with any of this?"

"Maybe nothing, maybe everything." Newberg shrugged. "That's what we're trying to establish."

"Wait, I thought the purpose of my being here was only to provide you with my statement."

"Yes, and you have been giving us your statement." Newberg shrugged again. "We're simply asking you some additional questions for the sake of adding some clarity and context to a few of the details in your statement, that's all."

"When we looked up your parents in our database," Browne paused to whistle, "all kinds of red flags came up. There were several redacted lines, and even more blocked information. Now, I find that fascinating."

"So *very* fascinating." Newberg nodded.

Alyssa nearly choked on the water she was sipping. "Hang on, am I a suspect in this case?"

"No," Newberg grinned. "Right now, you're an interesting person, not a person of interest. Yet."

Browne pulled out one of the chairs and sat down. "Listen, when I see a file like your parents have, it usually means one of three things. The person is either involved with the military, the national security services, or they're part of some high-risk operation."

Newberg saw Alyssa's confused expression, so he added some additional details. "You know, they could be an informant in a gang or crime syndicate, they could be a key witness in an upcoming federal trial, or something along those lines, where their information needs to be shielded from local police, in case there's a wayward cop inside the system."

"So," Browne leaned in, "are we close?"

"Even if you are right about any of those things," Alyssa looked from Browne to Newberg, "how is it relevant?"

"Another non-answer." Newberg clicked his tongue. "Did you catch that?"

"I did," Browne said. "It should be obvious why it's relevant, Miss Bristol. People with redacted files tend to be interesting people with an astonishing amount of very impressive enemies."

"And," Newberg interjected, "they tend to be the sort of very impressive enemies who could cause enough alarm in the people with redacted files to make them think they needed to take extreme measures."

Browne snapped his fingers. "Oh, you mean like bombing a courthouse?"

"Could be, yes." Newberg nodded in an exaggerated way. "So, let's review what we know. This year, you have been at the centre of an improbable number of extraordinary events, and yet you answer most of our questions with non-answers. So, either you are the world's most lucky – or unlucky, depending on your point of view – individual who just happens to be clueless, or there's something big and important you're keeping from us."

"So, how about you help us to help you by disclosing what's really going on."

Alyssa covered her face with her hands. "I don't want to talk about this anymore."

Newberg guffawed. "I can certainly understand why you don't, but how about I switch hats and see if I can assist in your defence."

Her hands dropped. "How?"

Newberg shrugged. "There must have been other staff in the mailroom with you while you were doing your own copying job. You mentioned Ashley, who we spoke with earlier. Was she, at any point, within reach of the box?"

"No, not at any point."

"And who else was there?"

"Aside from Ashley and I, there was Colin, Sylvana, and Melody."

"Were any of them near the box?"

"Not really." Alyssa frowned. "The copier is on the other side of the room from where Colin and Melody sit."

"And Sylvana?"

"Sylvana brought me the tape gun to seal the box, and she stood at the box for about one or two seconds, just to set the tape dispenser there." Alyssa took another sip of water. "She then asked how the job was going and wondered aloud if I needed any help."

"Okay." Newberg made a note. "And did she have any time near the box while your back was turned?"

"No, she was within my line of sight the entire time."

Newberg wrote more notes, then looked up at Alyssa. "Did anyone else come within three feet of the box?"

"The mailroom door is right beside the counter where the box was, so a few people were at least that close as they came in and out."

"Did any of them stop at the box, or did they all just walk past it?"

"Everyone walked past it, except for two people."

"And who were they?"

"Sylvana, who I just mentioned, and Gail was the other."

Newberg twirled his pen in his fingers. "And who is Gail?"

"She's the assistant to the lawyer whose copying job I was working on. She walked into the mailroom and told me she had brought me a label for the box."

Newberg noted and nodded. "Gail, okay, got it. We'll need to get her statement as well. And what is Gail's last name?"

"Whitmore. Gail Whitmore. She assists Sal Zanetti, a senior lawyer here."

"Thank you. And did Ms. Whitmore have any time alone with the box while your back was turned?"

"Maybe three seconds, if that." Alyssa paused to sip more water. "She came in as I was starting the job, so the box was still empty at that point."

"Hang on a second." Browne tapped his finger against his chin. "Why did she bring you a label?"

"I'd never been to the courthouse before, so Gail offered to make an address label for me, which had the room number and directions on it. That way I would know exactly where to go once I got there."

Browne thought for a moment. "And how long was she near the box in total?"

"Maybe ten seconds, tops."

Newberg made another note. "After she left, did you look inside the box?"

"Not immediately, no, but I was just finishing binding the first document, so I placed it inside the box a few seconds later."

"And there was no bomb inside the box at that point, correct?"

Alyssa nodded. "That's correct. It was completely empty at that point."

Browne folded his arms. "Is there any chance you're forgetting anything?"

"Like what?"

"For example, is there a chance that while you were at the courthouse, the box could have been switched out by someone?"

"No." Alyssa shook her head, her eyes locking with Browne's. "Unless the victims did it themselves, but that would make no sense. Like I told you, I took the box directly to Courtroom Twelve and delivered it into Mr. Richardt's hands."

"Did he say anything to you when you gave him the box?"

"Just a quick thank you, and the man beside him nodded at me."

"And then what?"

"And then *nothing*." Alyssa looked at both men. "I left the courtroom with the dolly to head back to the firm. I only made it as far as the hallway when I heard the blast."

Browne nodded. "We saw the courtroom security camera footage before we came here this morning, and it supports your description of the events, but..." Browne stroked his chin and stared at the floor for a moment. "There's something I'm still not understanding, so maybe you can help me with it." He then locked eyes with Alyssa. "Why did you take the box to the courthouse in the first place?"

"But I already told you why." Alyssa blinked at him, her expression morphing further into a look of complete confusion. "They were going to need those documents as soon as the lunch recess ended."

"No, you're not understanding what I'm asking you." Browne put his hands on his hips. "I want to know why you didn't send a courier to deliver the box. Wouldn't that be the standard way for a law firm to deliver time-sensitive documents to court?"

"I don't know. Probably. The documents urgently needed to be delivered, so I just took them there myself."

Newberg made a note. "So would you agree the boxes could have been delivered by a courier just as easily, if not easier?"

"Yes, if I had thought to call one."

Newberg looked up from his notes. "It would have been much easier for you to send a courier, yet you insisted on taking the box there yourself. Is there anything else you'd like to add?"

Alyssa shook her head. "I can't think of anything right now."

"Miss Bristol." Newberg pointed his pen at her. "In light of everything disclosed in your statement, you are both an interesting person *and* a person of interest in this investigation. You are not to leave town, and I'm serious about that. If you leave town without my direct, written consent, I will make it my life's mission to have you up on felony charges for doing so. Is that understood?"

"Yes." Alyssa shuddered.

Browne nodded. "Then I think we're done here for now, but you should know I'll need to speak to you again when I have more questions, and that will be sooner, rather than later. When that occasion arises, the questioning will take place at the police station, so I strongly suggest you obtain legal counsel between now and then."

Alyssa swallowed hard. "I understand."

Newberg stood up and looked at Alyssa. "Just wait here a minute." He walked over to the far corner of the room, pulled out his older-model flip phone, and punched in a number.

"Jesus, Richard." Browne rolled his eyes. "I thought the captain gave you a new phone to replace that old one."

"He did, and the new phone's in my desk drawer, safe and sound. Do you mind? I'm making a call here."

1:36 p.m.

Abby Lunay pulled open the thick glass door and then stepped inside the office tower's lobby. She watched from a distance, as the person she had been following pressed a button to summon an elevator.

Abby brushed aside a lock of her blonde hair, which had fallen into her eyes. It made her remember she was overdue for a haircut, but Alyssa had made Abby promise to never again use a hunting knife as a trimmer. Barbers and stylists were a waste of money, as far as Abby was concerned, to say nothing about how much time it took them to do a simple trim.

And boring.

It was so boring to just sit there, especially when Abby was used to haircuts being a two or three minute affair. She would sharpen her knife blade, and then a few swishes and hacks later, her hair was done. If she had to choose between styled hair which took an hour, or a quick cut which was practical yet failed to adhere to the conventional aesthetic standard, Abby would be sharpening the knife blade before the question had been completely asked.

The ding of the elevator snapped Abby back to the present, and she watched as her target stepped into the elevator with two other people. Once the doors had closed, Abby walked over to the banks of elevators and stared at the numbers above the elevator door, in order to see where it stopped.

The digital display over the elevator paused for a few seconds at number fifteen. Abby glanced at the directory. The fifteenth floor was home to an insurance company. It then continued up to the seventeenth floor, the main floor of the firm Dryden-Halbeck, and paused again. The elevator then began its descent back to the ground floor.

Abby nodded, knowing which of the floors her target had most likely gone to. Out of a sense of safety and discretion, she estimated she should wait at least three minutes before pushing the button to summon the next elevator.

1:37 p.m.

Newberg flipped his phone shut and then put it back into his shirt pocket.

Alyssa watched him. "Why are you looking at me like that?"

Newberg whistled. "It looks as if you're going to need that legal counsel even sooner than we thought."

"Why?" Alyssa wrinkled her forehead. "What are you saying?"

"I was speaking with my Lieutenant, and I explained the situation to him." Newberg shrugged. "The bottom line is he wants us to bring you in right now."

"What?"

"Alyssa Bristol, as per the standards and criteria in the *Anti-Terrorism Act* and the *Public Safety Act,* I am placing you under arrest on suspicion of committing an act of domestic terrorism, as well as two counts of murder. You have the right to retain counsel without delay, though this could be revoked if we find reasonable grounds to suspect your involvement in a pending terror plot. You also have the right to free and immediate legal advice from duty counsel by telephone. Do you understand what I have said to you?"

Alyssa felt her heart pounding, causing her head to throb. "I understand the words you're saying, but I'm not understanding what's happening."

"It should have been clear when I told you just ten seconds ago. What's happening is you're being placed under arrest and I'm informing you of your rights. Under the Acts I cited, you can be held for up to seventy-two hours without charge, however we are required to bring you before a judge within twenty-four hours of this arrest. Although section seven and section 11c of the *Charter of Rights and Freedoms* states you are not obligated to say anything, this is not a right you have under the *Terrorism Act*. You would, however, still have the right to an attorney. Anything you say or do may be used as evidence in court. Do you understand?"

"I think so, yes." Alyssa felt dizzy, and she was breathing heavily. "I want to call my parents."

"Not at this time." Newberg shook his head. "Under the Acts cited, we have the right to restrict who you can contact. If we suspect you have knowledge of a terror plot, you will be forced to give evidence to us in a court of law, even if you are not personally involved. Ms. Bristol, I'll need you to stand up and face the wall, as we're required to handcuff you before we escort you out of here."

Meanwhile...

Krissa Novak stepped off the elevator, turned to her right, and strode toward the reception desk. She was within an inch of being six feet tall, with fair skin and pale-blue eyes. Her short, sandy-brown hair was mostly obscured by a stylish dark grey bucket-shaped hat. Despite the summer temperatures, she wore a long, thin, light-grey overcoat.

"Good morning," Krissa flashed a wide smile at the two receptionists. "My name is Cheryl Hartman, and I'm here to see Sal Zanetti."

One of the two receptionists smiled. "I'm sorry, Ms. Hartman, but Mr. Zanetti is not in the office today. Did you have an appointment?"

Krissa frowned. "No, I just need to pick up a package from him. Could I maybe see his assistant Gail Whitmore? I can get it from her if it's easier for everyone."

"So sorry," the receptionist grimaced, "but Gail is also unavailable. There is a temp working at her desk today. I can call her, if you like."

"No, that won't work, as I will need to see Mr. Zanetti urgently if the package isn't there. Are you sure he's not here, or Gail?"

"Yes, unfortunately, neither of them are in today. Would you like to leave me with your business card or phone number so I can pass your contact information along to Mr. Zanetti when he calls in for his messages?"

Krissa pointed to her left. "His office is just down the hallway there, so I'll just quickly see if he's left it out on his desk for me."

"I'm sorry, Ms. Hartman, but we're not able to accommodate you in doing that, but I'd be happy to check for you if you'd like."

"No, it's okay. No need to trouble yourself. I'll just be ten seconds."

"Ma'am, I understand your concern, but you can't be wandering around like that." The receptionist stood up and walked over to Krissa and stood in front of her. "Again, I'd be happy to have someone check for you, it's no trouble at all. I can also try to call Mr. Zanetti and ask him about it for you."

"Is this how you treat his clients?"

"Our clients are made aware of how seriously we take their privacy." The receptionist's smile remained, but her brow was furrowed. "There are privileged documents sitting out on desks being worked on, so we can't allow anyone to go anywhere unescorted. I'm sure you understand."

"Listen to me very carefully," Krissa said in a low voice to the receptionist. "You're forcing me into taking a series of actions which I had hoped to avoid. You will not enjoy them, so unless you want your regrets to begin and your day to be completely ruined, you should make your way back to your desk, sit down, and let me take a quick look in his office on my own."

The second receptionist slowly reached under the desk and pushed the silent alarm button.

1:39 p.m.

The elevator door opened and a security guard stepped into the seventeenth-floor lobby. He was a man in his early sixties, who had seen all kinds of strange happenings in his decades on the job. Every day, it seemed, he was needing to deal with aggressive panhandlers, people with mental health issues screaming at passers-by outside the front door, or stressed out people who had suddenly snapped and felt the need to act out.

He saw two women arguing in the reception area. *Unruly visitor,* he immediately ticked off the appropriate box on his mental checklist. *Seems to happen every full moon.*

It was a stark and amusing contrast for him to behold, as one woman looked fit, tall, and presented as an imposing figure, while the other woman standing in front of her was at least a head shorter, but appeared fiery and defiant.

"Ahem," the guard pretended to clear his throat. "What seems to be going on here?"

The receptionist pointed at Krissa. "This woman is trying to trespass, and she just threatened me."

The guard began to approach Krissa. He, himself, was close to the same height as her, but had a stocky build, so he walked toward her with a swagger. "How about you and me talk this over on our way back down to the main floor?"

Krissa turned to face the guard. "How about no?"

Her arms moved in a blur. One arm struck out, and knocked the guard off balance, while she retrieved a firearm with her other arm from underneath her coat and hit him across the face with it, causing him to spin to the floor.

She then swung the handgun toward the receptionist, who stood wide-eyed and immobile.

"Step aside. *Now.* I won't ask you a second time."

The receptionist retreated to the front desk and dove underneath it, where the other receptionist had ducked into considerably earlier. Krissa was about to begin her march down the hallway, when she heard the security guard behind her.

"Code three," he shouted into his radio. "Lockdown protocol. Code three."

Krissa turned and pointed her gun at the guard. "Run. I'll be shooting in three seconds, so I suggest you run quickly."

The guard surprised himself at how spry he could still be, especially on such short notice. He sprinted through the reception area and headed, huffing and puffing, toward the exit stairwell.

"Three," Krissa said as she fired into the wall. She then pulled out a second handgun as a few people had begun to show up in the reception area to see what the loud bang was. Upon seeing the firearms, there were multiple screams, followed by immediate and panicked retreats. She made her way down the east wing, heading toward the corner office at the end, where Sal Zanetti's office was.

Along the way, a lawyer stormed out of his office and shouted at her. "You're not supposed to be here, so get out before I call the police."

Krissa fired a shot into the ceiling and then leveled the gun at his chest. "The next shot hits you in three, two…"

The lawyer reversed himself into his office, as though attempting a speed record for *sudden backwards leap*. The back of his legs hit the edge of his desk, and he fell backwards over top of it and he landed heavily upon the floor.

Meanwhile...

Detectives Newberg and Browne looked at one another.

"That sounded like gunfire." Newberg wrinkled his forehead in confusion. "What the hell is going on out there?"

Browne looked at Alyssa and then back to Newberg. "I can't help but feel that whatever is going on out there is somehow related to who we have in here."

"Yeah, I'd agree with that assessment."

"Whatever's going on, I don't want her getting shot." Browne led his handcuffed suspect to the end of the room and set her down on the floor behind the boardroom table. "Keep your head down and stay here until we check it out."

"Don't move." Newberg pulled out his handgun. "We'll come and get you as soon as it's safe."

Meanwhile...

Abby Lunay exited the elevator on the seventeenth floor, and she stepped out into the reception lobby of the law firm Dryden-Halbeck. There were the sounds of shouts and chaos in the distance, so she knew she had picked the correct floor. She strolled toward the reception desk which, to her surprise, didn't have anybody sitting behind it waiting to greet her. She stood in front of the desk for a moment, wondering what she should do, when she heard an argument coming from under it. The voices were female.

"You're on the Health and Safety Committee, aren't you?"

"What does that have to do with anything?"

"Didn't you learn how to handle emergency situations?"

"It's a committee. We discuss topics and eat muffins, like most committees do. Can you think of a single problem in the world that was solved by a committee?"

Abby walked around the reception desk and squatted in front of the two arguing figures, huddled together underneath it.

"You know," Abby looked at them, "when you're back here, your clients can't see you. It's not very receptive of you, especially considering this is a reception desk."

"That's because we're scared and we're hiding," one of them replied. "And you should be hiding as well."

The other woman spoke up. "Yeah, some lunatic is shooting up the place."

"No," Abby shook her head. "Most of my friends over the years have been lunatics their whole lives, and none of them would have acted out violently like that. Have either of you seen Alyssa Bristol?"

"Alyssa? I think she's still in the boardroom behind you, just over there."

"Thank you," Abby smiled and then stood up.

"Get down," one of them hissed. "She might see you."

"Who?"

"The crazy woman with the gun."

"No, it's okay." Abby smiled. "I doubt she's here to see me, or she wouldn't have come here in the first place, because this isn't where I'd normally be."

Abby walked over to the boardroom, which was about ten steps from the front desk. Abby opened the door and poked her head inside.

"Yo, Alyssa. Are you in here?"

"Abby?" Alyssa's head popped up from behind the table, as if she were a gopher. "What are you doing here? Who's shooting? What's happening?"

"That's way too many questions, and I've already forgotten the first one you asked." Abby then began to wave her arms, as though erasing an invisible blackboard. "No, wait. It doesn't matter, because I'm here to get you some place safe, so any questions you have will have to wait anyway. Come with me."

"It's kind of hard for me to stand up with these cuffs on."

Abby stepped over to where Alyssa was on the floor. She retrieved two thin, metal pins from a pouch on her belt and poked around inside the locking mechanism. Within seconds, the cuffs opened, and Abby pulled them off and let them drop to the floor. "There." Abby helped Alyssa to her feet. "Now let's go."

1:41 p.m.

Newberg pulled out his radio. "Dispatch, this is Fourteen. Send a tac-team and backup to the seventeenth floor of 1075 West Georgia, and I mean like yesterday."

"Copy that," the voice on the other end crackled. "We have reports of shots fired near your location."

"Yeah, you think?" Newberg scoffed. "We're not *near* the shots fired, we're *in the middle of* the shots fired. There's a Caucasian female, between five-ten and six feet, early thirties, with two handguns."

"Copy that. We're sending units. ETA, eight minutes."

"I copy. Out." Newberg put his radio away and shook his head at Browne. "Eight damn minutes. Do you know how much damage will be done by this maniac in the next eight minutes?"

"There's still too many civilians to risk taking a shot, and we don't have our vests on." Browne looked around. "Until backup arrives, we need to focus on getting everyone out of here before we attempt to arrest her."

The two crouched and hurried to the reception desk. When they arrived, they were surprised to see two women huddled together underneath.

"You ladies shouldn't be here." Browne looked from one receptionist to the other. "Both of you, get yourselves to the fire exit stairs. If you pass a fire alarm, pull it, so we can get the building evacuated."

1:47 p.m.

Abby and Alyssa burst out of the rear door of the building and into the loading bay. The elevators had been shut off, so they were both breathing heavily after having hurried down the seventeen flights of stairs. Abby led Alyssa to a car waiting off to the side. The driver's side door opened, and a large, stocky man with a beard stepped out.

Abby approached him. "Hey, Ryan. I got her."

Ryan nodded. When Abby got close enough, she tackle-hugged him. Ryan held her tight, then gently set her down.

"What's going on up there?" Ryan's deep voice rumbled. "The police scanner said there were shots fired."

"Don't know, don't care." Abby shrugged. "I got Alyssa out of there, so that's the main thing. Alyssa! Over here for a sec."

Ryan nodded at Alyssa as she approached. "Hello again."

Abby smiled. "Alyssa, you remember Ryan, right? He's the bouncer and bartender at Marcus' place."

"Yes, I do."

Ryan raised his eyebrows at Alyssa. "Are you okay?"

"Sorry, but at the moment, I really doubt it." Alyssa clutched the sides of her head with her hands. "Can either of you tell me what's going on?"

Abby thought for a moment. "No." She held up a finger. "Wait here a sec."

Abby walked with Ryan back to his car. Ryan patted Abby's shoulder. "You'd better get moving, my friend."

"I know. Thanks, buddy."

"Listen, Abby." Ryan frowned. "Be smart, okay? You've crossed Marcus, so he won't care if you're his niece. That's not going to protect you from this. He'll be hell-bent on finding you, and I don't see him being in a forgiving mood when he does. You might have burned that bridge permanently."

"I know."

"I'm worried about you, Abby." Ryan glanced over to where Alyssa was standing, then back to Abby. "You've gotten into this way too deep."

"I have to do this, Ryan." Abby sighed. "She's my friend."

Ryan scoffed. "No friend is worth getting killed over."

"She is."

Ryan's frown deepened. "You know what kind of people Alyssa's parents are, right?"

"Yeah."

"She's probably going to turn out like them, and I know you don't want that."

"Not really, no." Abby made a sour face. "But I'm starting to get used to them, and they've been really nice to me lately, so I guess it wouldn't be all that bad. Anyway, I don't care about any of that right now. All I know is I'm liking my life for the first time, and I can't stand the thought of losing Alyssa. I always lose everyone I care about, and I'm sick of it. I'm not losing her, too."

"If I don't ever see you again, I want you to know something. You've been a good friend these past three years, Abby." Ryan mussed her hair with his hand. "I'm going to miss you."

"I'll miss you too, Ryan."

"And don't contact me until this is over, for both our sakes. I've helped you today, but it ends here, so whatever you do, don't tell me where you're taking her. As soon as I get back to the bar, I know Marcus will send me out to find you, and I'll have to do it. He'll know if I'm not putting in a hundred percent effort, so do your best to hide from me, no matter what."

Abby nodded. "I will."

"That means I'm not allowed to help you at all."

She rolled her eyes. "Yeah, I get it, Ryan."

"So, that means I'm not allowed to suggest you contact my friend Lily." Ryan pulled a business card out of his wallet. "I can't tell you to call her and tell her I sent you, and I certainly can't tell you how good she is at helping people get into Malaysia unnoticed, okay?"

"Thanks, Ryan, but I'm not going to need that. You've already done everything I needed you to do. Now go away, because I don't want Marcus hurting you."

Ryan hugged Abby. "And watch yourself. You're walking off the edge of the map on this one, so expect more trouble than usual."

"I know." Abby said once the hug ended. "Don't worry. I'll stay safe, or I'll die trying."

"That's *exactly* what I'm worried about."

Ryan stepped into his car and shut the door. Abby walked back to Alyssa and watched as Ryan drove away. The sound of sirens were gradually growing louder.

"Come on," Abby gestured with her head. "We need to move."

Alyssa looked at Abby with pleading eyes. "But where are you taking me?"

"Right now, it doesn't matter." Abby shrugged. "The immediate priority is to get you far away from here. Then, I'll need to hide you until I can figure out what's happening. Let's go."

They began to walk at a brisk pace out of the loading bay and then east along Melville Street. Abby spoke as they walked. "There's too many cameras on taxis and transit, so we'll have to travel on foot for the time being."

"Who's after me?" Alyssa appeared dizzy and disoriented. "I need a moment to process everything that's happened in the past hour."

"There's no time for that." Abby's eyes darted from one side of the street to the other, looking for threats. "You can process stuff later. Right now, I need to hide you, and there's only one place I can think of where nobody can get to you."

"And where's that?"

"I can't tell you yet."

"Why not?"

"Because you're going to hate it so much." Abby put her hand on Alyssa's shoulder. "I need you to trust me for now, okay?"

"Okay, but can you at least tell me how far away it is?"

"It's nearly fifty miles."

"What?" Alyssa halted, mid-step. "I can't walk fifty miles, that's crazy."

"Don't worry." Abby pulled Alyssa forward so she'd resume walking. "We're not going to walk the entire fifty miles."

"Oh, that's good."

"At some point, I'm going to steal us a series of cars so we can get to where we need to go quickly and undetected."

Alyssa frowned. "That's less good."

"From here, it's around thirty miles to the American border, so we'll ditch the first car close to there."

"The border?"

"Yeah, we'll have to sneak across in a tunnel I know about, and then I'll need to steal a second car to get us the last twenty miles."

"But I can't do that," Alyssa wailed. "The police detective told me I can't leave town, or I'll be charged with a felony."

"I did say that you'd hate it so much." Abby looked into Alyssa's eyes. "Listen, someone went into the firm you work at and started shooting, so it's possible somebody is trying to kill you. With that in mind, ask yourself if you'd rather be a live felon or a dead suspect. Seems like an easy choice to me."

"There is so much wrong with this plan. I need to call my parents."

"Oh, that reminds me." Abby held out her hand. "I need your phone for a second."

Alyssa handed her phone to Abby, who then threw it violently toward the paved ground, then proceeded to stomp on it until it was in pieces. She then looked up at Alyssa and smiled. "Thanks. I almost forgot about that."

Alyssa's mouth hung open. "Why did you do that?"

"The first thing anyone trying to follow you will do is track the GPS chip in your phone. As soon as it's safe, I'll reach out to your parents on a burner phone. Come on."

2:25 p.m.

"This is terribly disappointing." Sal Zanetti sighed into his phone from the backseat of his car. He was being driven north along Granville Street toward downtown. "I had hoped to avoid this sort of outburst."

"Outburst?" Malcolm fumed into the phone as he paced the floor of his living room. He had put the call on speaker so Mary, who was typing feverishly at her laptop, could listen in as well. "You calmly inform me that a gunman shot up the firm and Alyssa's missing, and you're referring to my shock and surprise as an *outburst?*"

"It's precisely as I told you," Zanetti's voice carried the slightest of tremors. "What I know at this time is that two police detectives were taking Alyssa's statement, and were in the process of placing her under arrest, when –"

"Yeah, and about that," Malcolm interrupted. "How did the interview go so quickly from *hey, we're just taking your statement* all the way to *hey, we think you're a dangerous terrorist and need to be arrested immediately?*"

"I was neither at the firm today nor privy to the discussion the police had with Alyssa. Thus, I have no way of knowing the answer to your queries at this time."

Mary stopped typing. "Let me just clarify something. Are you saying people were being questioned by police detectives in the firm and there were no lawyers present to represent them?"

"Collecting witness statements does not require legal counsel, and that was what we were led to believe was taking place in the boardroom. Had I known there was any sort of formal questioning taking place, or that a statement could lead to an arrest, then I most certainly would have insisted that Alyssa – and everyone else, for that matter – be accompanied by an appropriately qualified lawyer, or a team thereof."

Malcolm put a hand on his hip. "Go back to the part where some lunatic came into the firm to redecorate the walls with bullet holes. You seemed to be implying she wasn't there for Alyssa. How can you be so certain?"

"Based on what I have learned so far, the alleged shooter—"

"Alleged?" Malcolm shouted.

"If I may continue without any further interruption, yes, the *alleged* shooter did not appear to be aware of Alyssa's presence. The suspect's priorities were focused on others."

"And yet," Malcolm grumped, "Alyssa went missing immediately after the shooting incident, so doesn't that seem like an incredibly odd coincidence to you?"

"My personal interpretation of what is or is not odd and coincidental is irrelevant and pure conjecture at this point."

"Don't give me that evasive legal bullsh…" Malcolm glanced at Mary. "Don't give me that *pile of bovine excretions.* With everything Alyssa's been through this year, I can certainly see her wanting to run away when the shooting started, but if she had done that, then she would have contacted us by now, and she hasn't. Our daughter wouldn't vanish into thin air without first letting us know she was okay."

Zanetti scoffed. "Your use of the term *vanished into thin air* is as hyperbolic as it is inaccurate. Aside from informing you of the events which recently unfolded, I was also calling to inform you that I have been told an unidentified woman whisked Alyssa out of the building, and I was told Alyssa appeared to be accompanying this person willingly. I have already called the security desk and demanded any footage they have of whomever took Alyssa, as well as of the alleged shooter. I shall pass anything relevant along to you."

"I'd sure as hell hope you would." Malcolm took in a breath. "Sorry, but I'm still trying to take this all in. I do appreciate you reaching out."

"Hold on," Mary looked up from her laptop. "Uncle Sal, can you hear me okay?"

"Indeed."

"I've finally managed to access the VPD's police dispatch message board. Let me read what was reported. The two detectives at the firm were onsite at the time of the shots fired report, and they described the shooter as a female between five-foot-ten and six feet tall, early thirties, and carrying two handguns. Four minutes later, they reported that the suspect had evaded capture, and their theory is she slipped out through the fire exit stairs during all the chaos, and then walked out of the building at the same time the tactical team was entering. There was also a brief message exchange, presumably about Alyssa. They said they had arrested a suspect on an unrelated matter and had them handcuffed."

"She was handcuffed?"

"Yes, Malcolm, but empty handcuffs were retrieved from the boardroom where Alyssa was being kept."

"Wait a second," Malcolm wagged his finger. "Alyssa can't pick locks."

Mary continued reading. "According to the message board, Alyssa was extricated from police custody by someone, and she is being reported as a fugitive at large. Dispatch has informed all units and regional police forces that... oh my."

Mary covered her mouth with her hand.

"What?"

Mary's hand dropped and her voice shook. "They alerted all officers that their suspect, Alyssa Bristol, is to be presumed armed and dangerous, as she is a suspect in a domestic terror incident which killed two people."

"Dammit," Malcolm fumed. "So any cops who see Alyssa will draw their weapons, so we're just one nervous twitch away from disaster. Jesus, talk about the presumption of guilt."

Zanetti sighed. "Your summary, regrettably, appears to be accurate. I shall endeavour to get more details of the terrible events which took place, and I will let you know what I discover. I am on my way to the firm as we speak."

2:31 p.m.

Marcus Coltrane waved at the chair in front of his desk and Ryan sat in it. Ryan had never seen Marcus looking this tired before, and it was unsettling that his usually unflappable boss appeared flapped.

"What's up, boss?"

Marcus rubbed his eyes. "Ryan, I'm going to get Darla to cover your duties at the bar for the next little while, because I need you to track down Abby. It'll be your main focus. In fact, I want it to be your *only* focus."

"Sure thing, but you could have just asked me that question out at the bar."

"No, because I want you right here in private when I ask this next question," Marcus looked into Ryan's eyes. "Is hunting Abby going to be a problem for you?"

"No." Ryan shook his head. "Abby and I are close friends, but business always comes first, you know that. In a case like this, you and the bar get priority."

"I'm glad to hear it." Marcus began drumming his fingers on his desk. "Any idea where she is?"

"No," Ryan replied sincerely, "but Abby's a creature of habit. She has routines she needs to follow in order to function. I've got this. I need you to trust me when I tell you I'll find her."

"I have good reason to trust you." Marcus leaned back in his chair. "So far, Alyssa hasn't reached out to your friend Lily, and as long as she doesn't, you'll maintain that trust."

"Ah." Ryan shifted in his seat. "How long have you known about Lily?"

"Since that time I asked you to eliminate Mr. Wong. Imagine my surprise, a few months later, when I learned he was seen in Kuala Lumpur, looking quite unexpectedly robust and alive."

Ryan shrugged. "You wanted him gone, and I made that happen. He hasn't been a problem to you since, and he never will be."

"I let it slide that one and only time, because I knew I'd given you a task you weren't comfortable doing." Marcus scowled. "It's forgiven, but it won't be forgotten. You owe me, big time. And just for your information, so there's never again any confusion about what I'm asking, when I say I want someone gone, I mean I want them no longer breathing, and never walking the earth again. There's no nuance, and it's not open to your personal interpretation. If I say to get rid of someone, you don't just send them off on some Asian holiday, are we clear?"

"Yeah, we're clear."

"Then let me also be clear about this." Marcus tapped his fingertip on his desk. "If Abby won't finish the job I sent her to do, then I'd prefer you to bring her in with near-fatal injuries."

Ryan shook his head. "No, you can't be serious about that."

"I am most definitely serious. There has to be a price paid for defying my instructions. That, and I find people are more receptive to my interrogation techniques when they're severely injured and in need of immediate medical attention."

"Come on." Ryan stood up. "This is Abby we're talking about. She's worth a lot more to you alive and healthy."

"I agree, but she's hasn't been the same since that pint-sized pest, Alyssa Bristol, came into her life. So, if my choice is to have Abby dead, or to lose her to Alyssa and her parents, then it's an easy choice for me."

"Look, Marcus," Ryan began pacing back and forth. "You know me. I'll get the job done, but I'm going to bring Abby back here alive and well, so this can all get sorted out over a friendly conversation."

Marcus sighed. "Listen, if she fully completes the job, then I'll be open to *possibly* sorting things out with her over tea and biscuits, if that makes you happy. But if she hasn't, then there'll be no options for niceties, as I'll have no further use for her."

"She'll finish the job." Ryan exhaled, then shook his head. "I'll find her and make damned sure she finishes it, okay?"

"I'm sure you will, because you know the type of measures I'll take if you fail. You've never let me down, buddy," Marcus winked. "Don't make this the first time."

"I won't disappoint you, but Krissa Novak will."

"How do you figure?"

"Because," Ryan sighed, "you can pay the Novaks to initiate violent acts, but there's no amount you can pay to get them to stop."

2:44 p.m.

Mary walked out of the bathroom and back into the dining room, blotting her eyes with a tissue.

Malcolm looked at her with concern. "You okay?"

"It was a spontaneous cry, but I'm feeling more composed now," Mary took a deep breath and let it out.

"You sure?"

"Yes, but if I'm going to stay composed, I'll need to be busy and focus on finding Alyssa."

Malcolm put his arm around her. "I think we can best do that by figuring out what happened and why it happened, and then from there, we can figure out where the hell she is."

"Let's review what we know." Mary cleared her throat. "A gun-wielding assailant went into the firm, intending an act of violence. Alyssa was either taken or rescued by an unidentified woman. Alyssa has not yet contacted us, and the GPS in her phone is either disabled or broken."

"Which likely indicates she is concerned about being tracked," Malcolm muttered while his mind raced. "And she could be laying low for now until the suspect is no longer in play, which I taught her to do."

"We also know she was in the process of being arrested. She went into the boardroom as a witness giving a statement, and she left the boardroom as a terror suspect."

"That about sums it up, yeah."

Mary frowned. "Our daughter just happened to be arrested at the same moment the shooter came into the firm. I can't help but connect the two events in my mind."

"Yeah, that much is certain, because otherwise, it would have to be one hell of a coincidence."

"Exactly, because she... wait, hang on a minute." Mary froze in place, her index finger raised. "What if we're missing the obvious?"

"We do that all the time, so it would be just a regular day."

She wagged her raised finger. "What if the courthouse bombing had nothing to do with securities fraud or domestic terror, and neither Richardt nor Zanikker were the bomb's intended targets? What if they were just collateral damage?"

"But who else was there?" Malcolm shrugged. "You think someone was after Judge Blanchett?"

"If they wanted her dead, then they wouldn't have had the box delivered and subsequently detonated during the court recess." Mary exhaled sharply. "And the bombing was too elaborate if the goal was simply to put a scare into someone."

"But who else was there, aside from a bailiff or some random spectator?"

"I'm thinking it's possible the target was, somehow, Alyssa. What if our daughter, the person carrying the box, was the target?"

A confused look appeared on Malcolm's face. "But it results with us having the same question. Why did they not detonate the bomb earlier? If they wanted her dead, then they missed their shot."

"Unless it was never intended to kill her."

"But why would anyone target Alyssa? And for that matter, *who* would target her?"

"Disgruntled members of the Zanetti family in Washington State. Henry Castle tried to kidnap Alyssa a few months ago, so it could be people aligned with him."

Malcolm glanced up at the ceiling. "Yeah, I suppose."

"Or anyone who's unhappy with us..."

"Okay, but aside from those additional *eight million people,* who else?"

"There's also the Russians." Mary shrugged. "They might have somehow figured out we helped Yuri defect last month in Panama, and this could be their way of getting back at us."

"Okay, fine, you've made your point. Alyssa *could* have been the indirect target of the attack as a means to get to us." Malcolm shook his head and whistled. "Jesus, if this bombing is about us, then there's so many new possible angles to consider, and so many new suspects who would have both means and motive."

"After everything that's happened this year, I certainly don't think it's an angle we can rule out."

"Yeah, you may be right about that." Malcolm thought for a moment. "We sent one of Sal Zanetti's relatives to prison for a thirty-year-old murder case, so, you're right, even someone inside the family could be behind this. We also made sure Henry Castle was sent away to a lovely future of solitude in a Supermax prison in Colorado, so he could have any number of people on the outside looking to make a statement on his behalf, and the shooter seems like the kind of person Castle would know. Hell, even Marcus Coltrane is unhappy with Alyssa and us, so he could be doing something."

"But we need the *why*." Mary looked at the ceiling as she thought. "It doesn't appear someone screwed up in the detonation, so Alyssa was meant to survive the blast. They specifically waited for her to deliver the bomb, which ended up killing two people, and they wanted her to survive. Now, who benefits from Alyssa having a close call? Oh, wait a minute. What if...?"

"Jesus, don't leave me hanging like that." His eyes widened. "What are you *what iffing* about?"

"What if the person or persons who orchestrated this carried it out in order to keep you and I distracted?

An attempt on our daughter's life would get us completely fixated on dealing with that, so we wouldn't notice anything else which was playing out at the same time." Mary locked eyes with Malcolm. "What if this entire thing is an elaborate misdirection?"

"Misdirection would fit what few clues we have, so you could be right about that as well. But still… this is one hell of a lot of work just to be a distraction. Okay, so let's think it through. Any idea what someone would want to distract us from?"

"Based on the bomb itself, and the complexity of what's happened thus far, my guess would be an upcoming terror attack."

"Yeah, I was already thinking about the terror angle as well." Malcolm pinched the bridge of his nose. "There's also no shortage of unhinged people who feel wronged by the courts, and a handful of them could possibly know about us. I can see one or more of them doing something like this to get to us."

"Exactly." Mary poked at the air with her finger. "So, even if she was the target, Alyssa could simply be an incidental in all this."

"Yeah, we should go on the assumption she's at or near the centre of whatever the hell this is. That way, we've got the bases covered, no matter what it turns out to be. We need to be prepared for the worst, just in case this involves us." Malcolm exhaled a long, slow breath. "Okay, so if you're right about this, then where would Alyssa be?"

"I don't know yet, but I know who can help us find her."

"Who?"

"Abby Lunay, of course."

Malcolm briefly cast his eyes heavenward. "Listen, Abby's great and she's proven herself beyond anything I ever thought she could, but in a situation like this… I just think it would be better for me to reconnect with some of the *morally flexible* contacts I used to run with way back in the day."

"No, you closed the door on that part of your life decades ago, and it's a door that needs to stay shut. Abby is the person we need. She has the loyalty to Alyssa we require, as well as her willingness to engage in ambiguous legality when it's needed."

Malcolm raised an eyebrow. "You're choosing to describe Abby's lifelong accumulation of felonies as *ambiguous legality?*"

"Yes, because if I dwell too much on the thought that I'll be giving indirect consent to her inevitable crime spree once she's hired, I'll go crazy."

"Fine, then I can live with the phrase, but there's something bugging me as well." Malcolm made a face. "Hiring Abby means giving money to Marcus, and I hate every atom and cell in his body. He also possesses one of the world's most punchable faces."

"Then you need to determine how important Alyssa's protection is, because we need Abby, even if it means handing money to Marcus. Marcus may be an enemy, but whoever is after our daughter is a bigger enemy. And isn't the enemy of your enemy your friend?"

"No, the enemy of my enemy is still my enemy, but you've made your point." Malcolm glanced at Mary. "If we're hiring Abby, then I don't want to be the one to deal with Marcus, because I won't be able to control myself."

"You have more self-control than you realize. You can be very polite when you decide to be."

"I can be polite around him, that part's fine. It's the nausea and disgust I won't be able to control."

Mary shook her head and sighed. "Fine, I'll make the call."

Mary pulled out her phone and selected Marcus' number, which she had saved. She held the phone against her ear, waiting for her call to be answered. The call was connected after the second ring. The voice on the other end was gruff. "What?"

"Hi Marcus, it's Mary Bristol, and I'd…"

"Where the hell is Abby?"

"I was phoning you to hire her, and I wouldn't be doing that unless I thought she was with you."

"If your daughter is taking up Abby's time, then I'll be sending you a bill."

"And then my husband will return it to you in person, and likely try to insert it somewhere, but none of this posturing is going to get us anywhere." Mary paused briefly, then resumed speaking. "I think it's safe to say, based on our conversation so far, that neither of us know where Alyssa and Abby are."

"I couldn't possibly care any less about your daughter. Abby is the only one who matters to me. I need her to finish the job I sent her to do, but instead I suspect she's wasting time with Alyssa."

"Seriously?" Mary scoffed. "An incomplete task is your big concern right now?"

"Yes, it seriously is my biggest - and only - concern right now. And frankly, my concerns are none of yours."

"Except for the fact that it would be wise for us to combine our efforts and work together on this."

Marcus made a sound of disgust. "And how did you come to that idiotic conclusion?"

"Alyssa and Abby are friends, and if they've both gone missing at the same time, then it's logical to assume they may be together. That means when we find one, we'll likely find the other."

"I'm well-aware of that, but it's still not advisable for us to collaborate. We'll be employing vastly different methods and tactics in our searches, and they won't be compatible. I'm sure your daughter's fine."

Mary rolled her eyes. "I don't know how Alyssa can be fine, when she's suspected of terrorism and murder."

"Then the apple didn't fall far from the tree, did it? You and your husband set the example, and now your daughter is following in your footsteps. You must be so proud."

"That's…" *unfair,* Mary was about to say, until she was struck with the worrying thought that it was at least possible he was partially right. They had exposed her to danger. They had overwhelmed her with information over the past few months about the secretive side of their lives. What if it had been too much for her to absorb? "Look, if something bad happens to Alyssa, then it may also happen to Abby."

"Then that's the chance we'll have to take, isn't it? I'm at peace with letting the chips fall where they may, but are you?" Marcus heard the silence at the other end. "Yeah, I didn't think so. And now you understand why we won't be working together on this. So, unless you want me to start charging you for my time, this conversation is over."

"Just one last thing. If you do find Alyssa, can you contact me?"

"Yeah, I will. I'll let you know." Marcus sighed, then answered in a softer tone. "Listen, I really do hope your daughter is okay, but don't call me again."

2:51 p.m.

Ryan scrolled through the data on his laptop screen. He had signed into his work account through an online portal, and he was looking for any clues as to where Abby might have gone. He had found an entry for a withdrawal of two-hundred dollars from petty cash by Abby, and she had left a note promising to pay it back.

Two hundred. Ryan made a face. *She won't get far on that.*

While scrolling through the expenses, he noticed another recent transaction for a significantly larger amount, and it sent a chill down his spine. It was marked *retainer,* but it was the payee Ryan was concerned about.

He pulled out his phone and tried to call Abby, but there was a recorded message indicating the number was no longer in service.

"Damn it, Abby." Ryan shoved his phone back into his pocket. He stood up and paced back the floor for a few moments while his mind raced.

He cursed under his breath. He knew whenever Abby was worried about being tracked, she wouldn't have her cell phone with her. She'd only be using burner phones until this was over, so he couldn't even alert her about what he had learned.

Ryan tapped his chin with his fingers, wondering where Abby was most likely to go. He mulled over his thoughts on this for a few moments, but then froze. It had occurred to him that his thinking was backwards. Abby knew he was tracking her down, so she would not go to any of her usual places. Instead, she'd go some place she normally wouldn't.

Ryan resumed pacing, and he went through his mental list of the places Abby often went to, and then tried to think of the places he wouldn't normally even think of her being.

A minute passed, and then another, until he once again stopped mid-pace. His eyes widened.

Of course, he thought. *She'd go to the one place she once told me she'd never go back to.*

Ryan grabbed his laptop, a few papers, and his keys, then ran out his front door to his car. As he opened the driver's side door and stepped in, he muttered under his breath.

"Abby's going home."

2:59 p.m.

Mary paused her frantic research on her laptop, and looked over at Malcolm. "What was that grunt about?"

Malcolm slouched at the dining room table, fingers pinching the bridge of his nose. He had been poring over the bits and pieces he had available to him pertaining to his daughter's predicament and he sighed, then looked back at Mary. "I've looked at the evidence they have, and Jesus, it's a lot. I mean, it's all circumstantial, but it all connects, and there's so damned much of it. How are you holding up? Are you doing okay?"

"Not really, and I'm trying to avoid thinking about it, so please don't ask again." Mary resumed her work. She was attempting to track Abby's phone and find clues as to hers or Alyssa's whereabouts, but had, thus far, been unsuccessful. "Sorry, but like I told you earlier, too much has happened, and I haven't had time to process everything, and I can't afford to be processing right now, or I'll start to panic. So, let's both think. In light of what Marcus said, it stands to reason the woman who took Alyssa away is Abby."

"I agree, but what does Abby have in mind?" Malcom leaned back and stared at the ceiling. "What's her plan? Where would she take Alyssa?"

"She may not have a plan." Mary's phone began to buzz. She looked at the screen to see who it was, but it simply said *private caller*. She decided to answer it. "Who is this?"

"Hey, Mary, it's Abby. I'm on a burner phone, which is why you didn't know it was me."

"Abby, I'm so glad you called. We need to talk."

"I know, and I'm sorry I drank your entire bottle of wine at Alyssa's eighteenth birthday party last week, okay? But she ran out of my medicine, so I had to."

"No, I don't care about that right now." Mary put the call on speaker so Malcolm could hear. "I need to hire you."

"You'll have to go through Marcus, because I'm not allowed to freelance. Actually, wait. I might not even be working for him anymore, so I don't know how hiring me works. I'll need to think about that."

"Please, just give me thirty seconds right now, that's all I'm asking."

"What do you want?"

"Alyssa's been framed for murder, and now she's missing. I don't know where she is, but I'm assuming she's with you."

"Yeah, I know where she is, and that's why I was phoning you in the first place. I wanted you to know she's safe."

"Can I speak with her?" Mary failed to keep the urgency out of her voice.

"No, I can't have anyone tracing this call."

"I'm begging you to listen to me, Abby," Mary pleaded. "I've done hundreds of phone traces. My phone is encrypted, and all but untraceable. It would take an expert several hours to track it."

"Fine," Abby groaned. "Thirty seconds and no longer." She passed the phone to Alyssa.

"Mom?" Alyssa immediately burst into tears. "I'm so scared."

"Can you get to me?" Mary sniffed. "Your father and I will hide you."

"I… I don't…" Alyssa tried to catch her breath in between sobs. "I don't think I can."

Abby patted Alyssa's shoulder. "We have to go. Now."

"Mom, I'm sorry, but I'll try to talk to you again as soon as it's safe. I love you."

Abby took the phone. "Don't worry, Mary. I'm going to hide her where nobody can get to her."

"Where are you, Abby?" Mary wailed. "Please, her father and I can help you."

"I know you can. But I also know you'll be able to help me a lot more if I *don't* tell you."

"Um…" Mary paused to see if she could fully understand what was just said. "That doesn't make any sense to me."

"Maybe not," Abby sighed, "but it makes perfect sense to me. Bye."

"Abby?" Mary shouted.

Malcolm pointed at her phone. "Can you trace the call?"

"With the limited equipment I have to work with?" Mary scoffed. "No chance at all. Any idea why she thought I'd be more helpful if I didn't know where Alyssa was?"

"I gave up trying to get into Abby's head a few minutes after I first met her. I never thought I'd meet someone with a more chaotic mind than mine." Malcolm rubbed his chin. "Hang on a sec. I have a theory. It's possible Abby was being evasive because either she thinks our phones are tapped, or we're being watched."

"The detectives," Mary nodded, and glanced at her phone. "That's a possibility, and it does fit with Abby's secrecy. In that case, we're back to doing our own research. What have you found out so far?"

"I contacted my security guard buddy in the Court Registrar's office. He scanned and emailed me the preliminary report the police gave his boss about the bombing. The bomb was detonated remotely. The receiving device was about the size and thickness of a quarter, it's professional-level. And the explosive used in the blast? It's a special variant of C4 plastic explosives. One or two ounces would have been enough to kill both men, but the report estimates eight to ten ounces were used."

"Which means they used a lot more than they needed." Mary nodded. "Any idea why they would do that?"

"If it wasn't such a clever attack, I'd guess they didn't know what the hell they were doing. But this," Malcolm whistled, "this wasn't some clumsy, half-assed bombing, which therefore implies the excessive amount was intended. I mean, Jesus, the top half of the box left a small dent in the ceiling tiles of the courtroom. Using the amount they did tells me they not only wanted to kill people, they wanted to make a big flashy statement."

"Any idea what statement the bomber was trying to make?"

"Aside from *I'm a violent bastard,* no." Malcolm sighed. "But, as it happens, I am quite familiar with this variant of the explosives."

"You are?"

"Yeah, when I was assisting MI6 a couple of years ago, there were two underground armouries I saw which employed that specific variant of C4. One was in Belfast, the other in Londonderry."

"Ireland?"

"Specifically, *Northern* Ireland, which got me to thinking… were either of the victims Irish or English?"

"From what I've learned so far, no." Mary shook her head. "By ancestry, Hans Zanikker was Austrian and Arthur Richardt was Dutch."

"Damn. So the type of bomb doesn't help us much. It only means our bomber was familiar with the methods of the IRA and UDA. Oh well, it was worth a shot. We need to find out who did this."

"We won't be able to figure out the *who* until we first figure out the *why* and the *how*."

"Well, the *how* can be figured out *after* we know the *who*." Malcolm looked at her. "We need to stop this bomber from harming anyone else, so right now the *who* is more important than the *how* or the *why*."

"But the *why* will lead us to the *who*, which is why the *why* is as important as the *how*." Mary folded her arms. "I don't know where to look for the *why,* or what the *how* will end up being, but I'm certain the *what* and the *how* will lead us to the *why,* which will give us the *who.* Are you having as much trouble following this conversation as I am?"

"Yeah, and I'm getting a headache from it. I've been hearing some awful stuff about Zanikker. Apparently, he was a real piece of work, so I'm sure there's any number of people who could want the bastard dead."

"That wouldn't surprise me." Mary huffed. "Have you seen some of the terrible things he posted on his blog and social media pages?"

"I never look at social media, so I assume your question was rhetorical. What sort of crap did he post?"

"There's all kinds of white supremacism nonsense, and that's just scratching the surface." Mary wrinkled her face in disgust. "A lot of his content was either bigoted or homophobic, but the vast majority of it was appallingly racist. After seeing it all, I'm surprised Mr. Zanikker didn't spell his name with a third *K*."

Out of the corner of her eye, Mary noticed movement on her laptop screen, which was showing the footage from the hidden camera facing the front path. She looked at the image.

"There's two men in suits coming up the walk"

"Is it those Jehovah's Witnesses who keep coming here? I wish they'd stop bothering me."

Mary gave him an incredulous look. "They might stop bothering you if you'd stop arguing with them."

"I'll stop arguing with them the minute one of them can tell me why their book says there's a mandatory death penalty for eating shrimp, but enslaving your neighbours is perfectly okay."

"Please don't start all that dissecting of Biblical quotes again. I just got rid of the headache I had from your *where did all the water go after the Great Flood* argument. Oh, and it's a moot point, because these are definitely not Witnesses."

"How do you know?"

"I see police badges on their belts. They're detectives."

"Damn. I'd definitely have preferred the Witnesses. Do you think it's the same two bastards who arrested Alyssa?"

Mary nodded. "There's a good chance it is, but either way, be nice."

"I'm always nice."

"Good point," Mary sighed. "I've seen your version of *always nice,* and it most often isn't. Maybe let me do the talking, okay?"

"Suits me."

By the time the men knocked at the door, Mary had her hand on the door's latch, and she opened it immediately.

"Hello," she looked from one man to another.

"Hello," Browne held up his identification. "I'm detective Browne and this is Detective Newberg. Are you the mother of Alyssa Bristol?"

"Yes."

Malcolm appeared behind Mary. "And I'm Alyssa's dad. What's this about?"

"We have some questions," Newberg said. "Has your daughter been home today?"

"No," Mary wrung her hands. "We're hoping to hear from her soon."

Newberg reached into his shirt pocket and pulled out a black-and-white picture and showed it to Malcolm and Mary. "This is an image from a security camera in the lobby of an office building downtown. It shows your daughter and an unidentified blonde woman. Do either of you know who that is?"

"Yes, we both know her," Mary shrugged. "She's a friend of Alyssa's."

Newberg retrieved his notepad and pen. "What's her name?"

"Abby Lunay."

Newberg wrote the name down. "Ms. Bristol, we have reason to believe Abby Looney is a threat to your daughter."

"It's L-u-n-a-y, *Lunay,* and I trust her," Mary leaned against the door frame. "Abby's always kept Alyssa safe, so I doubt she's a threat."

Newberg stopped writing and looked at Mary. "We have video footage of Abby Looney entering the lobby of the building behind the suspected shooter. The shooter gets on the elevator and Ms. Looney waits, then gets on another elevator three minutes later, to follow the shooter up so they can arrive at different times."

Malcolm folded his arms. "And what's your theory about why Abby would do that?"

"It seems self-evident." Newberg stared at him. "We have reason to believe the shooter went up first to create a diversion in order to draw us out, and then Miss Looney swept in to take Alyssa away. *Again.*"

Mary's eyes narrowed. "What do you mean by *again?*"

Newberg scoffed. "This isn't exactly your daughter's first abduction this year."

"Abby didn't abduct her, they're friends." Mary scowled. "If Abby took Alyssa, then it was only because she was trying to protect her."

Newberg let the words go around in his head, hoping they would make sense to him, but gave up. "If she was only interested in protecting your daughter, then wouldn't she have reached out to you by now?"

"She did, actually." Mary looked at him. "Abby called me nearly an hour ago to say Alyssa was fine, but she wouldn't tell me anything else."

"Where is she now?"

"I don't know."

Newberg pulled out his notepad and pen. "What number did she call from?"

"She called from a burner phone, so the number won't help you."

Newberg stared at Mary for a moment before speaking. "And it doesn't surprise you at all or seem suspicious to you *in any way* that the person who has your daughter is using *a burner phone?* Where were they calling from?"

"Abby wouldn't tell me."

"And you somehow don't find that alarming either?" Newberg's eyes bulged for a moment. "Seriously, what's it going to take for you to see that none of this is normal?"

"I'm not implying it's normal," Mary snapped. "I'm just trying to focus on the most important aspect of all this, which is finding my daughter."

"You're probably going to hate this, but I have to ask." Newberg put away his notepad and folded his arms. "How can you be sure your daughter isn't just acting out for attention? I mean, I understand she's been having some mental health problems. With everything that's happened to her these past few months, this could be some sort of cry for help."

"And there it is, folks." Malcolm sighed. "That's officially the stupidest, damned thing I've heard all day."

"Malcolm," Mary flashed a glare at him, then turned and glared at Newberg. "You think she's planning abductions and bombings just because she goes to a therapist? She's getting some assistance in order to help her deal with some post-traumatic stress caused by events which no young person should have to experience, but that doesn't automatically mean her mental health problems are severe enough to cause her to snap and violently act out. If anything, it's a positive sign of self-awareness and a desire to heal."

"Yes," Newberg nodded. "And also of a troubled mind."

"Keep that up," Malcolm sneered, "and you may end up troubled in a completely different way."

"Be careful who you're threatening, tough guy." Newberg looked down his nose at him. "I don't care who you are or what big-shot job you have. If either of you or your daughter cross a line, you'll be arrested. And, let me just add that right now, the only thing that would give me greater pleasure than slapping some cuffs on you is finding your daughter and putting her in front of a judge."

"We don't want trouble, honestly, we're just really stressed right now," Mary soothed. "All we want to do is find some answers."

"Speaking of wanting answers," Browne cleared his throat, "we've heard a story or two about you both when we were trying to look you up. I found them pretty hard to believe."

Mary nodded. "If they're the stories I'm thinking of, detective, then I'd probably find them hard to believe if I were you, too."

"Speaking of hard to believe," Malcolm interjected. "If you're such senior detectives, how come all you've managed to come up with so far are wild accusations and no hard evidence?"

Mary flashed a glare at Malcolm.

"Right." Malcolm sighed. "I'll be quiet."

"Now that I've met you," Browne studied Malcolm and Mary, "I think it's safe for me to assume you're not military, as you don't fit their profile. You're not likely protected witnesses either, because there's too much attention being drawn to you all. That leaves national security."

"We are involved with national security, yes." Mary nodded. "But it has nothing to do with our daughter or the bombing. She's just an innocent bystander in all this."

"Innocent bystander?" Newberg laughed. "Come on, cut the comedy routine. Just since the beginning of April, your daughter was kidnapped by a team of paramilitary mercenaries, she was nearby when a house exploded, was on the scene in a shoot-out, was outside the door of the courtroom where a bomb killed two people, then she was in the boardroom with us when some idiot with a gun started shooting up the office, and now she's on the run as a fugitive with someone using a burner phone. Are you seriously trying to tell me that her presence in each and every one of those things is just a coincidence?"

Malcolm raised his hand. Mary pinched the bridge of her nose, sighed, and then motioned for him to go ahead.

"Yeah, most of it is a coincidence." Malcolm folded his arms. "Now, let me tell you why."

"Oh, please do." Newberg put his hands on his hips. "I wouldn't miss this explanation for anything."

"Alyssa is a pawn in all of this." Malcolm's eyes went from Newberg to Browne, then back to Newberg. "Back in April, a group of criminals went after her as a means to get to us. We suspect that's what's happening here. She didn't bomb the courthouse, but it was made to look as though she did."

"For what purpose?"

Malcolm shrugged. "We don't know that part yet, but it may be to keep us busy while something else plays out. If that's the case, then it must be something big."

Browne squinted. "So, you have no hard evidence either, just speculation? Looks like having evidence behind a theory are only good enough when it suits you."

Newberg shook his head. "If you want us to believe this is all about you, then we're going to need a lot more from you than your speculation and wild-assed theories."

"Sorry," Mary said, "but you're going to have to settle for what we've told you, because that's all we're able to give you at this early stage."

"Then you'll have to settle for us being unconvinced." Newberg pulled out his notepad and pen. "Now, just for the sake of being able to identify your daughter if we see her, does she have any piercings or tattoos?"

Malcolm shook his head. "None that we're aware of."

"She'd better not have any." Mary added.

Malcolm looked at Mary. "Seriously? Didn't you say people with tattoos have the right to express themselves however they see fit, seeing as how it's their body?"

"Yes, but I wasn't including Alyssa in that."

"Are you aware—?"

"Yes, I know that makes me a hypocrite, so don't say it," Mary groaned. "Besides, you don't want her having tattoos, either."

"All I said was I could remember a time when tattoos were an act of rebellion and not conformity."

"Christ," Newberg moaned, loudly. "Are you two quite done?"

"Do you know what?" Malcolm snapped. "Yeah, we *are* done. I'm done with your speculation, done with your insinuations, and done with you throwing everything against the wall to see what sticks." He pointed above the detectives' shoulders toward the sidewalk. "I want you off of our property right now."

"We'll leave, but that won't end anything except this conversation."

Malcolm flashed a mirthless grin. "At this point, I'd count that as a win."

"You'll be wanting to cooperate, for your daughter's sake."

Malcolm pointed. "And you'll want to be leaving for yours."

Newberg winked at him. "We'll see you soon."

Mary and Malcolm watched from the door, as the detectives made their way down their front path and then to the sidewalk. Mary closed the door, then exhaled.

"Okay," Malcolm cleared his throat. "Before you say anything, I'm sorry. I know I wasn't nice at the end and I wasn't quiet."

"No, but it was absolutely perfect the way you did it." Mary smiled at him. "Thank you."

Malcolm smiled and hugged her, masking his bewilderment. *I will never understand women.*

3:08 p.m.

The two detectives walked in silence along 29th Avenue, toward their parked car. Eventually, Browne spoke. "That certainly didn't go as well as I'd hoped."

"Are you kidding me?" Newberg clucked his tongue. "It went even better than I'd hoped. I now know exactly what buttons to push in order to get results."

"What are you thinking?"

"We both know Alyssa Bristol is guilty of something, we just don't know exactly what yet." Newberg glanced at Browne. "The best way to resolve this is to go hell-bent after Alyssa, and, if we apply enough pressure, the parents will fold. Then we'll find out what's really going on."

Browne approached their vehicle, pondering what his partner had told him. "I don't know."

Newberg used his key fob to unlock their vehicle. "You got a better idea?"

Browne opened the passenger side door and stepped into the car. "Right now? In this weird case? I have no ideas at all."

Newberg sat down, closed his door, and started the engine. "Then let me handle this. I'll visit the parents tomorrow morning, and stir up a real hornet's nest."

August 18

Mary scoffed at the image on her screen, which was from the security camera aimed at her front yard. She scowled at the sight of Detective Newberg looking toward her home while also leaning on her front gate.

She wished Malcolm hadn't headed out to the bank, as he generally handled these situations with a complete lack of tact, which she felt would be appropriate in this instance. She groaned audibly.

Mary stomped to the front door, opened it, and glared at him. Newberg straightened up and gestured for her to come out to speak with him. Mary briefly considered making some gestures of her own, but instead opted to take the less-satisfying high road. She marched out, glare remaining in place, and strode along the front path to where the detective was standing. When she arrived in front of him, she folded her arms.

"Ms. Bristol," he smiled. "I just need a small moment of your time, please."

Her nostrils flared. "What do you want?"

"First of all," he sighed, "I'm sorry if I let my frustrations get the better of me yesterday. I was out of line, even though it had been a really long day."

Mary's glare relented, though only slightly. "It was a long day."

"Listen," Newberg spoke softly. "When I'm on a case, I know I can get a bit... *surly.* It's nothing personal, okay?"

When she nodded, he continued. "I just have a couple of quick questions for you. Are you okay with me asking them?"

"Go ahead."

He nodded. "You and your husband... you have top secret jobs, do I understand that correctly?"

Mary's eyes began to scan Newberg from head to toe. He noticed her studying him, so he followed up his own question. "I'm not wearing a wire or any other recording device. I swear on my badge and my life."

Mary nodded, then carefully chose her words before responding. "We're security consultants for some high-level clients including governments, so yes, in that sense you do understand correctly."

"Are you spies or something?"

"We're *something,* but that question is way above your scope and pay grade, regardless."

"I guess that's fair." Newberg narrowed his eyes. "I have a new theory, and I believe you'll find it interesting. You want to hear it?"

"Probably not, but go ahead anyway."

"Let's assume, for the sake of argument, you *are* a spy or some kind of spook." Newberg put his hands up. "Just for pretend, okay?" He let his hands fall back down to his sides. "Now, imagine you were given the hypothetical mission of killing someone, but you couldn't, for whatever reason, be the one to actually carry out the assassination yourself. It would be a genius move to get your daughter to deliver the bomb for you."

Mary shook her head and scoffed. "If you somehow think it makes sense that a mother would jeopardize her daughter's safety like that, then you're too stupid to be a detective."

"Ah, but *you* would be the one controlling the detonation device in that scenario, wouldn't you?" Newberg raised his eyebrows. "So your daughter wouldn't be in any danger at all. And remember, this is all just hypothetical for now, okay? Now, think about it. She delivers your explosives, it goes off, and it looks as though some enraged investor - or one of the defendant's other scam victims - delivered a little payback. Nobody would ever suspect the young woman. She'd appear to be an innocent victim because nobody would know about her connection to you and your spy job, but she'd actually be, at best, an unwitting accomplice in your actions. What do you think about that?"

"I think it's obvious to me you have no leads, no clues, no credible theories, and you watch too many crime shows on TV." Mary's glare re-intensified. "I also think it's a really good thing I'm going to continue conducting my own investigation, as the last drop of faith I had in you has now completely evaporated."

"That's rich."

"What I said was rich? What *I* said?" Mary blinked at him. "Are you serious? Physician, heal thyself."

"Like it or not, Ms. Bristol, your daughter is, *at the very least,* an accomplice to a major crime. At worst, she's a killer and a terrorist." Newberg let his words settle in Mary's mind before continuing. "Either way, she's on a path to prison, unless you cooperate."

"You're wrong on both counts," Mary snapped. "Alyssa is innocent."

Newberg folded his arms. "Then what about Sal Zanetti?"

"He's not involved in this." Mary's indignation was somewhat derailed by the sudden and unexpected mention of her uncle. "Why would you ask me about him?"

"Because in order to make sense of what's happening, I need to know why the shooter at the law firm was targeting him."

Mary's eyes widened and her mouth briefly hung agape. "Wait, are you saying he was the assailant's target?"

"Huh." A wry smile appeared on Newberg's face. "You didn't know that, did you?" His smile broadened. "I find it so very interesting that your uncle didn't tell you that."

"No, he didn't." Mary attempted to continue speaking, but couldn't find the words. She closed her mouth and then made a second attempt. "What are you even saying to me?"

"When the shooter went into the firm, she specifically asked to see Sal Zanetti." Newberg watched and studied her facial expressions as he continued. "When told he wasn't in, she asked to speak with Gail Whitmore, his assistant. When informed neither were in that day, our suspect forced her way into his office with guns blazing. She assaulted a guard, trashed your uncle's office, and then shot some holes into the walls and ceiling for good measure." He saw genuine confusion on her face, which made him chuckle. "I can't believe this. There was a serious and violent armed attack at his place of work, and yet your uncle didn't think it worth bringing up to you, *his own niece.* Huh. Somehow, your family is even more screwed up than mine. This case keeps getting stranger by the minute."

"I don't know what to say to that, but I'm going to have a serious chat with him about it, and he won't enjoy it at all."

Newberg smirked. "Yeah, you probably should speak with him, because it looks like I'm not the only one Sal Zanetti is hiding things from."

"Apparently not."

"Any idea what the shooter might have been looking for in his office?"

"No, sorry, I don't." Mary's voice was now softer, as her mind raced with these new revelations. "This is all new information to me."

"I'll be in touch when I have enough to present my next set of questions." Newberg looked at Mary. "Though somehow I think you have even more questions at the moment than I do."

"You're probably right about that."

"Listen, Ms. Bristol... eventually, we are going to find your daughter. And when we do, we'll have no choice but to file enough charges against her to put her away for a very long time. The sooner you decide to help me, the better this is going to play out for everyone. Think about your daughter's future."

"I am thinking about it."

"So, is there anything you'd like to tell me?"

"Yes. *Goodbye,* Detective Newberg."

10:19 a.m.

When Malcolm returned home from the bank, Mary brought him up to speed on every aspect of Detective Newberg's visit, including the unexpected bombshell.

"Jesus, you mean the shooter went to the firm looking for your uncle?"

Mary nodded. "According to Detective Newberg, yes. And she also asked for Uncle Sal's assistant."

"And your uncle somehow didn't think any of that was worth mentioning to us?"

"Apparently not." Mary sighed, then looked at Malcolm. "Why are you making that face?"

"Because I can't imagine why the hell anyone would launch a violent attack against a dull, long-winded Wills and Estates lawyer."

"Aside from the obvious, I don't know."

Malcolm's brow furrowed. "What's the obvious?"

"There are two victims in the bomb attack, and it's reasonable to assume they both had wills."

Malcolm thought about her words for a moment. "Good point. And that means there might be something in one or both of those wills which is worth killing for. If the bomb was about somebody's will, then it might actually have been coincidental that Alyssa was there at that time after all."

"It's possible."

"Yet I still find it highly improbable." Malcolm scowled. "Something still doesn't feel right. I just don't know what we're missing, but my gut tells me it's something big."

"Then I suppose I need to go and find out what it is." Mary grabbed her car keys.

"Where are you going?"

"I'm going to head out to Dryden-Halbeck to see Uncle Sal to ask him about the victims and their wills. The shooter was asking for him and he didn't tell us, which makes me wonder what else he's been keeping from us."

"Just phone him."

"No, he's less likely to be evasive if I'm there in person."

"Fair enough." Malcolm nodded. "You want me to go with you?"

"No, I'd prefer to handle him by myself."

"Okay, but while you're on your way there, how about I phone Sal and see what I can squeeze out of him ahead of you getting there? I'll call you after I talk to him and let you know whatever I find out."

"Why not? It can't hurt, I guess." Mary nodded at him as she headed out the door. "Good luck."

10:25 a.m.

"Enough of the games." Malcolm fumed, and he tightened his grip on his phone. "That gun-toting psycho was looking for you when she shot up the firm."

"Yes, so it would seem." Sal Zanetti made no effort to hide his impatience.

"And when were you planning on telling Mary and me that little detail?"

"I had no plans to disclose it to either of you at all."

"Why the hell would you keep something that important from us? Seriously, what reason could you possibly have?"

"If you wish to hear a reason, then I shall oblige you with three particularly important ones." Zanetti put Malcolm on speakerphone. "You are not leading this investigation, I have reasonable concerns you will compromise the police investigation, and it is vitally important everything be done correctly and I lack the confidence you will do so."

"You're as contemptible as you are stubborn," Malcolm snapped. "Mary and I are the best hope Alyssa has."

"Only if you succeed," Zanetti thundered. "One mistake or one careless misstep, and the guilty parties elude justice, and I shall not risk such an outcome, no matter how much it upsets the two of you."

"Then at least let me ask you this." Malcolm took a deep breath in order to help calm himself. "Who hates you enough to come into your workplace and unleash eight kinds of hell?"

"Prior to a month ago, I might have said you."

"Don't try to deflect the question back to me." Malcolm gritted his teeth. "It's time for full disclosure, because lives are on the line, so that means no more secrets, okay? Alyssa is missing because of this, do you get that? Did that critical piece of information get through your thick skull? This isn't some dull cross-examination in court, this is real danger to your actual family. So, with all that in mind, tell me why the shooter was asking for you."

"I swear upon everything I hold sacred that I have not even the faintest of ideas."

"You must've seen the security camera footage by now and looked at the assailant."

"I have, indeed."

"Then can you at least tell me who the hell she is?"

"With God as my witness, I had never seen that individual prior to this terrible incident. Whether or not you choose to believe me, it remains the complete truth."

"Let me state the obvious here," Malcolm raised an eyebrow. "You're an expert on estate matters, and now there are two dead people whose estates are coming into play. Are you saying the courthouse bomb and this nutcase shooter aren't somehow tied to you through your capacity as an estates expert?"

"In light of the details you have just stated, I suppose I can hardly blame you for asking that question," Zanetti's voice softened. "I can now better appreciate how you could have tied those events together to form that hypothesis in your mind. With that said, however, neither event connects to me in any way which I am aware of. I did not prepare the wills for either of the deceased men, though I did sign off on them as the department head."

"Then you have to be missing something in their estate documents."

"I am not one to overlook pertinent details in estate matters, so I can assure you that is not the case. Neither man's will was anything but ordinary and routine. There was certainly nothing in either of them which would be worth killing for."

"Even if there was, would you disclose the details to me?"

"Of course not." Zanetti laced the words with derision. "I would never betray the confidence of any document I signed off on. The only way to obtain those details would be through a court order or by getting the consent of the parties involved."

"Convenient," Malcolm scoffed, "especially when you consider they're both dead."

"Then a court order would be your only path forward."

"I don't believe this." Malcolm groaned. "Even when members of your own family are at risk, you're a stickler for every goddamned little rule. You are putting your paying clients above my daughter, and it makes me want to throw up. You stonewall me, but you give your paying clients whatever they want, no questions asked."

"I find your tone as offensive as your words are twisted," Zanetti huffed. "I am a well-respected lawyer and an upstanding member of society. My ethics are impeccable, so I resent you making me sound like some sort of common street prostitute."

"The two professions have more in common than you'd ever admit. You're both shunned by polite society and your clients pay a lot of money to get screwed."

"Your crass attempt at wit falls terribly short, as our clients pay us to *avoid* being the coital recipient."

Malcolm sighed. "Look, I know you're not a shark, though I only know that due to the absence of any obvious dorsal fin. I know lawyers are essential, because they ensure everyone has recourse to the law."

"I detect the imminent arrival of the word *but*."

"Yeah, *but* I also know lawyers are only as effective as the laws on the books. If we have unjust laws, then lawyers are there to ensure *injustice* is done."

"On that one point, at least, we agree." Zanetti gave a quick nod. "I assure you, every judge with whom I have ever shared a meal or had drinks wishes he or she could either adjust the laws or implement new ones, but such changes fall within the realm of politics, not law. Politicians write laws, lawyers test them, and judges both interpret them and ensure they're enforced. It's hardly a perfect system, but it has served this country well for over a hundred and fifty years."

Malcolm scoffed. "And I'm sure that brought so much comfort to women and non-whites for the first hundred of those years, but we're getting off track. I want to find out who would want to kill Richardt or his idiot client. Or both. Speaking of his client, what was your personal, off-the-record opinion of Zanikker?"

"Herr Zanikker was valued as a client, but as an individual, he was a contemptable and ignorant hate monger, so I genuinely loathed and despised the wretched fellow."

"Then it looks like we agree on a second thing."

"So it would appear. However, even a deplorable vessel of odious filth such as Zanikker is entitled to legal counsel when he has his day in court. As a client of the firm, we were obligated to do our duty and represent him, despite our unspoken revulsion of the man himself."

"Yeah, fine, I get it," Malcolm shook his head. "Listen, Mary will be arriving at your office shortly to talk to you further about this."

"There are no words to adequately express the level of excitement that particular thought brings me."

11:22 a.m.

"No," Zanetti looked over his reading glasses at Mary. "As I told your husband, there is nothing in either man's will which would be grounds for an assailant to carry out violent attacks of this magnitude or any other."

"May I see the wills?"

"Of course not. Client confidentiality supersedes your morbid curiosity, and I fail to see how that most basic of legal concepts continues to elude you."

"I asked to see them because there's something missing which might explain what's happening, and it may be in one or both of the wills." Mary paced in Sal's temporary boardroom office. "I can *maybe* buy you having no idea why the shooter was asking for you, but there must be a case you're working on, or a client, or something else which connects you or your assistant to the shooter."

"If indeed that is the case, then I promise you I have no knowledge of it, nor any clue as to what the connection may be."

Mary stopped pacing and looked at him. "Where's your assistant?"

"I advised Gail to take a leave of absence. She's distraught and devastated about Arthur's death, as I'm sure you can imagine. She's led a quiet life, free of the sort of incidents which occurred, and she has been left traumatized by it all. Her husband died three years ago, so she has no-one to make sure she takes the time to recover, so I personally assumed that responsibility."

"It was kind of you to do that," Mary muttered.

"It was the decent and honourable thing to do. Gail has been my loyal assistant for so long, she's like family to me, so it therefore behooves me to ensure she is looked after."

Mary paused to think for a moment. "Were she and Arthur Richardt particularly close?"

"Gail has worked here for over thirty-five years, so she views everyone in the firm as part of her extended family. Before she agreed to assist me, she used to be head of the Articling Student program, and she also looked after the first-year associates. Arthur Richardt was just one of dozens of lawyers she's known since their start at the firm. She was like a mother hen with each new batch of law students."

"She sounds like a remarkable person."

"She is, indeed." Zanetti removed his reading glasses and set them down on his desk. "A handful of staff – Gail, Teresa, Dimitri, Donna, and Nasrin – have been with the firm since its earliest years. They're the pillars of the firm, and Alyssa met each of them in her first week of employment. Donna is the backbone of the firm – the first and only administrator we've had here. Teresa does all the staff hiring, and she's very selective.

Dimitri's been our head of Accounting since day one, Nasrin is our indispensable head of IT Services, and of course Gail has run the Articling Student program since we were a seven-lawyer firm."

"I'd actually like to ask you about the client who passed away. Why was he in court?"

"He was being accused of Securities Fraud and related improprieties."

Mary pulled out a chair and sat down. "Sorry, but isn't Securities Fraud a *criminal* matter?"

"Yes, of course it is."

"Then I'm not understanding why a *corporate* lawyer like Richardt would be assigned to a *criminal* trial?"

"As I mentioned prior, the accused was a client of ours, and Richardt is – or rather, he *was* – the head of our Banking Department. He was an expert in the field of Finance Law, so he was there to assist lead counsel with the defence. He was set to provide testimony as an expert witness."

"So then who was lead counsel for the defense?"

"Antonio Bellantoni."

"As in my second-cousin Tony?"

"Yes, but he prefers Antonio. He feels *Tony Bellantoni* sounds too much like a whimsical name in some trashy piece of fiction."

"Why wasn't Antonio in court when the bomb went off?" Mary grimaced. "Wait that sounded terrible the way I asked it. I mean, thank goodness he wasn't there, but... why was Mr. Richardt there and not him?"

"Antonio informed me he had stepped away to deal with an urgent matter, but he had been in the courtroom all morning and was scheduled to be there for the rest of the day as well. Arthur only stayed behind during the lunch break so he could brief the client about what to expect once the trial resumed."

"That makes sense," Mary nodded. "I have some questions for Antonio, so I'll need you to give me his contact information."

"I shall do no such thing, as attempting to contact him would be futile."

Mary blinked. "Why?"

"Antonio is a police witness in a criminal investigation, so I have already advised him to refrain from discussing the incident with anyone, *especially* you and your husband. He's the criminal law expert, not I, and he has agreed this is an appropriate measure under the circumstances. Although he has no fear of what may unfold, I have advised him to only answer his phone if it is me calling, and that he should avoid going back to his home or place of work until further notice, as a precautionary measure. He is going along with it in order to put me at ease."

"It's vitally important that I speak with him." Mary stood up. "Alyssa's safety may depend upon it."

"I worry deeply about Alyssa, and I pray she is safe and remains as such, but you may not speak to

Antonio at this time. I shall respond harshly if you attempt to do so."

"You're being impossible."

"Perhaps I am being impossible, but you are being reckless, which is far worse."

"In your opinion." Mary folded her arms. "Okay, I have a question about the day of the bombing. Do you happen to know what was scheduled in the trial for that afternoon?"

"To the best of my knowledge," Zanetti leaned back in his chair, "they were going to delve deeper into Securities Law. Arthur was going to testify as well as assist Antonio with the content."

"About Mr. Zanikker, the defendant. If he was being accused of securities fraud, then I imagine he made some enemies because of that."

"He most certainly did." Zanetti steepled his fingers. "Aside from the fraud charges, he was also facing a class-action lawsuit."

"I assume his investors were angry about him running off with their money."

"Allegedly."

"*Allegedly*, of course." Mary rolled her eyes. "But would you have a guess as to how many of those investors would want him dead?"

"I would suggest to you that most of them would want him dead, so your question is not the pertinent one. What you need to ask is how many of the investors would want him dead badly enough to send a bomb into a court room, and the answer to that question currently eludes me."

"Just to give me an idea about the scope of this, how many investors were allegedly defrauded?"

"Seven-hundred, forty-one."

Mary whistled. "That's a lot more than I was anticipating. That sure is a large pool of angry people to select a suspect from."

"It was a mutual fund, so consider it fortunate there were as few as that." Zanetti leaned forward. "Funds of that nature can often involve *thousands* of investors. In this particular fund, some people had a few hundred dollars invested, while others had a few hundred *thousand* dollars invested. The fund held more than four million dollars, and only one million of that sum has been recovered thus far."

"Then maybe we should be focusing on the people who lost the most."

"Not necessarily." He picked up his reading glasses and used them to point at Mary. "A multi-millionaire who loses a hundred thousand dollars is more likely able to absorb the loss than some working-class person, whose ten-thousand dollar life savings just disappeared."

"I suppose that's true, which puts me back to square one."

"Square one?" Zanetti scowled. "You shouldn't be at any square at all. This is hardly some child's board game, Mary, it is a serious matter which is both outside

and beyond of your depth and expertise. Let those police detectives worry about finding the guilty party."

"So far, trusting the police has only resulted in Alyssa becoming their primary suspect in a domestic terror attack with murder charges pending, so forgive me if I'm choosing other options at the moment."

"My preference is for you to leave it alone entirely, at least for the time being. I shall continue to press the police to widen their investigative search and to clear Alyssa's name, while you should be more focused on your daughter's academic future, and not this tragedy."

"That's an impossible request." Mary threw her hands up into the air. "My daughter's academic future is shaping up to look more and more as though she'll be studying for exams in the prison library, so I'd rather not leave it in anyone else's hands, thank you very much. I'm involved in this, whether you like it or not, so accept it, and stop trying to get me to sit back and wait to see what happens next."

Zanetti stood up and leaned on the boardroom table. "As your uncle and head of the family, I forbid you from taking any further steps into this matter."

Mary mirrored her uncle's pose, and locked eyes with him. "As Alyssa's mother, I don't care what you forbid. You don't get the final say when it comes to the safety and well-being of my daughter."

"I find your emotional and irrational disposition both wearisome and repetitive. Are you quite done?"

"No, I'm just getting started. Now, tell me about Arthur Richardt. Did he have enemies?"

"Arthur?" Zanetti sat back down. "Heavens no. Unlike his client, Arthur hadn't an enemy in the world. He was a well-liked and well-respected colleague. He was a kind and decent fellow, who was even highly regarded by opposing counsels, no matter how heated the trials would get. Arthur did Finance Law, so the majority of his clients are – *were* – bankers, and they thought of him most fondly, because he saved them hundreds of millions of dollars over the span of his career."

"Was he an investor in the mutual fund?"

"No. He was simply the go-to person for banks whenever they were being sued."

Mary stood up straight. "Then doesn't that mean some of the people who had previously sued the banks and lost have potentially become his enemies?"

"Highly unlikely. They'd more likely direct their wrath and rage directly at the banks than whomever happened to represent them in court that day. Arthur would occasionally persuade the banks to pay a token sum to the groups of people suing them, when he felt it would help to smooth things over, so he was viewed as a fair man."

"Okay, that information helps me." Mary nodded. "Now I have to figure out what to do next."

"There is nothing further for you to do, so my suggestion to you is for you to put it out of your mind."

"I don't believe this. Your long-time friend and colleague was murdered." Mary let out an exasperated groan. "My daughter – *your niece* – is missing. I thought you'd welcome my help and would be wanting to collaborate on this, but instead you're doing everything you can do either block me or shut me down. Why is that?"

"As I have attempted to tell you numerous times already, and without success, I might add, *this is a police matter*. Until we have more facts and pertinent details, it is unwise for anyone, regardless of their good intentions, to interfere or to act prematurely."

Mary slapped her palm against the table. "Are you a human being with, like, actual emotions, or some mechanical humanoid incapable of feeling? Don't you want justice for your friend?"

"Yes, I most certainly do. In fact, right now, I want nothing more than to see justice for Arthur." Zanetti pulled out a handkerchief from his suit jacket pocket and blotted his eyes. "And that is precisely why I don't want any part of the police investigation being meddled with." He wagged his finger at her. "As for my feelings, yes, I do have them, and they pain me so, yet I do not allow them to guide my decisions. I do not want to see your name on a document which is being used to have the case against the bomber dismissed. Now, if you'll excuse me, I wish to head out for lunch. *Alone.*"

Sal Zanetti exited the restaurant and began his walk along Robson Street back toward the firm. He had managed only a few steps before he was approached.

"Sal Zanetti," Detective Newberg stepped out from around the shaded side of the restaurant. "A moment, please."

"I cannot spare a moment, especially for the likes of you, as I am in haste," Zanetti continued walking, not so much as glancing at Newberg. "I have meetings this afternoon which I need to prepare for."

"We can walk and talk."

Zanetti scowled. "I certainly can, at any rate."

"Listen, Sal – may I call you Sal?"

"You may not, and I trust you will forgive me if I shun you with as much contempt as I can muster."

Newberg raised his palms skyward. "What'd I do?"

"We agreed to let you take statements from witnesses, in an effort to expedite your investigation, and you turned it into a formal interrogation of my niece." Zanetti looked at Newberg. "The moment you attempt to press charges, I want you to know I will personally petition the court and argue your methods constituted entrapment."

"Listen, I really appreciated the cooperation of the firm, Mr. Zanetti, and nobody was more surprised than me at how things unexpectedly evolved. We were only interested in taking your niece's statement, but in the process of us asking her to elaborate on certain details, we established grounds for an arrest."

"Hmph," Zanetti looked down his nose at the detective. "It is my opinion that her arrest was neither surprising nor unexpected for you, which is why we rescinded our cooperation with the police. I trust you and the rest of the police force to conduct this investigation thoroughly and competently, but you shall have to do so without any further cooperation from us. Any additional questioning you wish to undertake or statements you wish to collect will occur only through a court order, and even then it will be attended by a team of lawyers, some of whom will be looking for even the slightest grounds to sue the city *and* the police for damages and a written demand for your immediate dismissal."

Newberg looked at him and smirked. "You think any of that scares me?"

"My objective was not to induce fear, it was intended to be taken as a statement of fact and of fair warning. Your callous insensitivity to the horrific incident we endured will not be forgotten."

"Hey, listen, if I came across as insensitive, I apologize. We're determined to catch the bomber and shooter, whether they're the same person or not, so everything I have done so far has been to achieve that objective. Believe me, I know this has been a difficult time for all of Mr. Richardt's friends, family, and colleagues."

"Indeed, it has."

Newberg cleared his throat. "It was so fortunate your niece and nephew were out of the courtroom when that bomb went off, wasn't it?"

"It was a blessed and fortuitous miracle, indeed."

"I think you picked the right word, there. It really was a kind of miracle. In fact, it's almost as if someone had been looking out for them."

"Ah, I see." Zanetti nodded. "Do go on and finish that thought." He then held up his right hand. "No, on second thought, allow me to finish it for you. You now appear to be speculating that I may have sent the explosive device, and somehow, against all rational probability, arranged things so that Antonio and Alyssa were barely spared, while Arthur, my dear friend and esteemed colleague of over thirty years, was killed, along with his client, Mr. Zanikker."

"I'm not speculating anything of the sort." Newberg held up his hands. "I'm just asking questions, so I can find out what really happened. That's what detectives do, you know. We ask questions and we figure things out."

"Yes, that is what *detectives* do; however, what you are doing more resembles someone in a fishing trawler. You're casting an absurdly wide net in the hopes of snagging *something* instead of *the right thing*. Standard police procedure these days appears to be more about quickly concluding each case, rather than ensuring justice is done."

"Not even close, and that's a pretty interesting statement coming from a lawyer. You know, all we cops do is follow the evidence, produce a list of suspects, and then apprehend the most likely culprits. It's up to you lawyers to ensure justice is done, not us. Don't they teach hypocrisy in law school?"

"No, that class was outsourced to the police academy. It's an elective every recruit is encouraged to take after completing *Entrapment 101* and *Faulty Reasoning.*"

"Tell you what." Newberg let out an exasperated sigh. "I'll stop taking cheap shots at your profession and you do the same, so we can focus on the case. You've seen the evidence we currently have, and we've also collected quite a few witness statements. Every single piece we've collected points to the same conclusion, so are you actually going to attempt to tell me it all *doesn't* point to your niece?"

"I would tell you no such thing." Zanetti turned to his right and crossed the plaza, leading to the office tower's front doors. "The few pieces you've cobbled together – and *poorly,* I might add – do, indeed, point vaguely in Alyssa's direction. What I am asserting is the bits you have are woefully incomplete. The so-called *cheap shots* I was taking were aimed at your apparent desire to stop looking for other possibilities now that you have a suspect who fits enough of the clues to satisfy you. To cease looking for other evidence and other possible suspects at such an early stage would be shoddy detective work. I am certain this is a contributing factor in the general public's increasing distrust of the authorities. I'd much prefer you did a more thorough job of analyzing your assembled evidence – and I use the word *evidence* rather loosely – from this point forward."

Zanetti pulled open the glass door and stepped into the lobby, and made a point of not holding the door open for the detective. Newberg caught the door before it closed and hurried behind Zanetti, following him to the elevators.

"Despite your holier-than-thou moral outrage," Newberg snapped, "you haven't given me one shred of information to address the obvious pattern of your niece's very recent history. She's been at the centre of a lot of, shall we say, *misadventures* in the past few months." An elevator opened and Sal stepped inside, Newberg at his heels. The door closed and the elevator began its rapid ascent. "Alyssa Bristol has been through more extraordinary events in the space of a few months than most people see over the course of their entire lives. Maybe you don't like the way we're interpreting the evidence we have, but frankly, there's no other rational way to look at it."

The elevator stopped and opened. Zanetti stepped out and Newberg continued to follow him.

Zanetti glared at him. "I have work to do."

"So do I, and mine is about murder, so it's likely more pressing than yours right now. Just answer a few more questions, and then I'll leave you in peace."

Zanetti stepped around the corner and proceeded down a long corridor. He turned to his left and walked inside a meeting room, which had been converted to into a temporary office.

Newberg stepped in and looked around. "You work in here? Isn't this a boardroom?"

"We are currently standing inside a space with the word *boardroom* on the door, so what it is should be self-evident, even to you. As for why we are in this space, I certainly did not come here in order to prolong this tedious conversation. You declared my office to be a crime scene, if you recall, and I cannot help but believe you would frown upon my attempting to use it to conduct business, so the answer to your first query should have been so obvious as to render it moot, and thus unnecessary to verbalize. For the time being, I need to work from here until my office is once again at my disposal. Are we quite done with your vapid questions?"

"Almost, but not quite. I want to know if there is anything else you want to tell us, which may assist us with this case?"

"Not at this time, no."

"Really?" Newberg's eyebrows went up. "Nothing at all?"

"If you wish for me to repeat myself, I shall oblige you one final time. No, there is nothing more."

"That's so interesting, because it means you're withholding vital information from me."

"Such as?"

"My partner and I spoke with both of the receptionists who were at the desk at the time of the shooting, and they both told us the shooter was asking to see you or your assistant."

"With God as my witness, I am getting a headache from needing to think down to your rudimentary level." Zanetti emitted a weary sigh. "Allow me to attempt to put this into words which even you can understand. I was informed you had already spoken with the reception team and I thus assumed you had already obtained that information on your own. It may have been an error on my part to assume you were neither incompetent nor a complete imbecile, but even a detective with room temperature IQ would have obtained that information. Thus, it would have been redundant for me to mention it to you again."

"See these?" Newberg pointed to the sides of his head. "These may look like ears to you, but they are actually highly-effective bullshit detectors."

"I shall attempt to keep my enthusiasm and awe at your grasp of vulgar metaphors to a mere minimum."

"Someone walked into your firm, asked to see you and your assistant, and then trashed your office while shooting up the place. That's a big deal to most people, and yet you just sit there, acting as if it was just another Tuesday."

"Do not allow my stoic exterior to lead you to make such erroneous assumptions. The safety and security of the firm and everyone who works therein is of the utmost importance to me. Detective, I often operate in court, occasionally in the presence of hostile opposing counsel, so I have made a habit of maintaining what is known in the vernacular as *a poker face*."

"Okay, I get it." Newberg nodded. "That makes sense, and I can accept that. So, how about telling me what the shooter was looking for in your office."

"If I had even the slightest idea what she was seeking, then I would inform you of it without hesitation.

The unalterable fact, however, is that I am bereft of ideas as to what the suspect was hoping to see, find, or acquire in my office."

"And that's everything you want to share with me right now?"

"I believe you have everything you need from me."

"Not quite." Newberg put his hands on his hips. "You see, I also happen to know you very recently obtained the services of a security company to patrol your house and to drive you to and from work."

"Yes. And what of it?"

"It implies you believe you're in danger. You don't think that's important for me to know?"

"Until I know what is happening and why it is happening, hiring security is a pragmatic and prudent precaution. It is a personal decision, and therefore hardly relevant to your investigation."

"Incredible." Newberg stared at Zanetti while his head shook. "Honestly, I'm really struggling to figure out how your brain works. What about your assistant? Did you hire extra security for her as well?"

"Her safety and security are of the utmost importance, so yes, I made arrangements for her protection as well."

Newberg narrowed his eyes. "What sort of protection did you arrange?"

Zanetti shook his head. "Until I know who can be trusted, I shall disclose no details about any of my arrangements."

"And your assistant's name is Gail Whitmore, is that accurate?"

"Indeed."

Newberg nodded. "I'll need to speak with her."

"Yes, of course. I'll arrange for an interview immediately."

"What, no argument from you? No push-back? That's a first."

"It was a logical and reasonable request for you to make. Gail was named by the assailant, plus she was in contact, albeit briefly, with the box you allege had explosives inside of it. Ergo, it's only prudent for you to ask her some questions pertaining to those matters."

"Great, then how about calling her into your office for a moment?"

"Unfortunately, Gail is not in the office, as I have put her on a leave of absence. I am willing to phone her for you, if that would suffice."

"For now, sure, it will *suffice* nicely."

Zanetti looked at his watch and then picked up the phone's receiver and punched in some numbers. He waited for the phone to be answered.

"Hello Gail. Yes, it is good to speak with you as well. How are you holding up? Yes, of course. I can only imagine. How is the family? Excellent. If you need anything, don't hesitate to ask. Where are you right this moment?" Zanetti nodded as she spoke. "Wonderful. Gail, I need to tell you something and I need you to listen carefully to every word I say. I'm calling you at your home because there is a police detective here who wishes to ask you some questions pertaining to the recent tragedy. Yes, precisely. I am putting you on speakerphone now, do you understand?"

Zanetti pushed a button on the phone and then cleared his throat. "Gail, I am joined on this call by police Detective Newberg. Can you hear me clearly?"

"Yes, I can hear you."

"Hi Ms. Whitmore, I'm Detective Newberg. Please state your full name for me."

"Gail Jessica Whitmore."

"Thank you." Newberg pulled out a chair and sat down. "I know this is difficult, as the events are still very recent, but I need your help to make sure the bomber doesn't hurt anyone else. Are you willing to answer some questions to help me out?"

"Yes, of course, dear. I'll do whatever I can to help."

"I appreciate that, Ms. Whitmore." Newberg pulled out his pen and notepad. "Now, your last contact with the box that was taken to the courthouse was when Alyssa Bristol was just starting to copy the documents, do I have that right?"

"Yes, Alyssa had mentioned she hadn't been to the courthouse before, so I made the dear girl a label for the box with directions to the courtroom for her." Gail audibly sighed. "And to think that young dear girl could have been killed. *Any* of us could have been killed. It's all so upsetting."

"Thank you, Ms. Whitmore, this is helpful to me." Newberg made some notes. "Did you notice anything unusual about the box when you came into the mailroom with the label?"

Gail began to sob. "I had no idea what was going to happen."

"I know, Ms. Whitmore, and I understand this is difficult for you. Just do your best."

Gail's sobs continued. Sal Zanetti's face wrinkled and he cleared his throat. "It's alright Gail. We can do this another time. For right now, get some tea and do your best to get yourself composed."

There were sounds of sniffles and a barely audible "Okay."

Zanetti disconnected the call. "My apologies, Detective, but my assistant is not in a sufficient emotional state at this time to be speaking with you and answering your questions. I shall make arrangements for another conversation for you with her in the near future."

"The *very* near future, I hope."

"Yes, of course."

"Can I get her number?"

"Perhaps at another more appropriate time."

"Okay," Newberg nodded. "But speaking to me will help her. We can't eliminate her as a suspect until we get our questions answered, so the sooner the better."

"Yes, naturally."

"Let me ask you this," Newberg stroked his chin. "Can you think of anyone who works here who would want your colleague or his client killed? Maybe a professional rivalry, bad blood, or anything along those lines?"

Zanetti shook his head. "The suspect you seek is unlikely to be anyone from the firm, as the deaths of Arthur and his client cause us more problems than solutions. Nobody gains, nobody benefits. Arthur was a highly respected mentor at the firm, not anyone's rival."

"I have to ask this, okay? What about your assistant Gail?"

"How would she benefit from any of this?" Zanetti's eyes narrowed. "She has no connection to the client, the judge, or opposing counsel. She's known Arthur since he was an Articling Student here, and they had an excellent professional relationship."

"Apologies in advance for this next question, but it also needs to be asked," Newberg sighed. "Was their relationship always purely professional?"

"Yes, it was always and only completely professional."

"Thank you." Newberg thought for a moment. "Was Gail an investor in the client's mutual fund?"

"Heavens no." Zanetti emitted a short laugh. "Her money has always been divided between a simple GIC and a savings account. She's far too conservative an investor to ever put her money at risk."

Newberg stood up and leaned forward, putting his fists on Zanetti's table. "Then what about you?"

"I lost a dear colleague and friend." Zanetti glared at Newberg's hands. "I gain nothing, as I am not in Arthur's will, I have no ill feelings toward our client, no matter how much contempt I have for his personal views, and I was not invested in the fund. And think of what I would lose if I did commit such a reckless and heinous act."

"Instead of asking me to think about it, how about you just tell me instead."

Zanetti scoffed. "My career and reputation would be ruined, and I'd bring dishonour, shame, and embarrassment to the family name, which is unthinkable to me."

"Is there anything else you want to tell me?"

"Yes, there are three final things."

"What?"

"The first is telling you to remove your hands from my working surface. Second, find your way to the elevators and remove yourself from this building. Third, do not bother me again, or I'll be explaining what constitutes police harassment to your captain."

Newberg met up with Browne at the end of the block.

"Well?" Browne asked. "Did you get anything?"

"Yeah, his assistant completely lost it when I mentioned the box."

"That's a red flag for sure."

Newberg nodded. "Based on her response and evasiveness, it could mean she's our bomber."

"Maybe, but it could also just mean she's a sweet old lady who hasn't been able to process everything she's been through."

"You going all soft on me?" Newberg scoffed. "She works for that stuffy bastard, so she's hardly some delicate flower. I think we need to push everyone even harder."

"You're already pushing the *Alyssa Bristol is probably guilty* angle more than you probably should."

"Trust me, it's the only leverage we have at the moment to force people to give us information. Like I've been saying, we know Alyssa Bristol is guilty of *something,* we just don't yet know what, so the harder we push in her direction, the faster someone else in her family cracks and either give us something useful or points us in the right direction."

"Yeah, you do keep saying that, but I'm wondering if you repeat it for my benefit or your own."

Newberg shrugged. "Maybe a bit of both."

"I hope you're right, because none of this adds up."

"Well, how can it add up when we can't get anything useful from anyone?" Newberg grunted. "Our primary suspect has vanished, her parents are giving us the runaround, the lawyer's being evasive, and his assistant can't be reached except through the lawyer. This whole thing stinks of being one big cover-up."

"Yes, and I can feel it in my bones." Browne put his hands on his hips. "That lawyer definitely knows something critical to our investigation, and he's going out of his way to avoid telling us what it is. Or maybe he's covering for his assistant. Either way, we may have to bring him in for questioning."

"Maybe," Newberg shrugged. "But we also need to talk to the parents again, because we still have too many unanswered questions."

"And you think they'll suddenly tell you something useful?" Browne looked up at his partner. "We need a break in the case, or we'll just keep spinning our wheels and getting nowhere. Any luck tracking Alyssa Bristol or Abby Lunay?"

"A few leads, but nothing has panned out yet. I have a source or two looking for them as well. They'll turn up. In the meantime, I need to turn up the heat."

2:02 p.m.

Malcolm approached Mary, who was working on her laptop in the living room. She looked up at him. "Did you speak to the boss?"

"Yeah, and let's just say it was a reminder for me about why I retired from this line of work." Malcolm pinched the bridge of his nose. "I explained Alyssa's disappearance and our current situation. Bottom line, the only help they'll give us is a leave of absence."

"But that can't be right. Our contract with them states we can get assistance whenever we're in danger or if there's a credible and actionable threat."

"Yes, *we* can get help, but it turns out that offer doesn't extend to our relatives or dependents."

"That's completely ridiculous," Mary scowled. "Once this is over, we're renegotiating that contract."

"Or terminating it."

"Renegotiating would be wiser, bearing in mind who we work for. Bottom line, though, is we're on our own with no resources."

"No, we have a ton of resources, if you think about it." He smiled at her. "We have a house full of materials, equipment, technology, and an array of gadgets. We have more than we need to conduct any operation on our own."

"True, so let's think for a minute." Mary stood up and faced him. "Who would go after Sal and his assistant, and for that matter, *why* would they?"

Both Malcolm and Mary recoiled in response to the sudden and loud impacts upon their living room window.

"Get down," Malcolm tackled Mary and both landed hard on the floor. Impact marks covered the intact window while the air was filled with the pulsating sound of a machine gun. A brief pause was followed by another spray, this time at other windows and the front door. These bullets weren't stopped, however, and the sounds of shattering glass, splintering wood, and divots in the wall were added to the existing cacophony.

Malcolm and Mary crawled on their stomachs across the floor, making their way around the corner, where the brick from the living room fireplace would provide them with some additional cover from the onslaught of lethal projectiles. Malcolm braved a glance around the corner toward one of the blown-out windows, and saw a solitary figure, clad in body armour, with a long, bulky machine gun.

"You know," Malcolm hissed, "I will no longer comply with your *no wearing guns in the house* rule. I hate not being able to shoot back."

"Do you seriously think your Beretta would be useful against our attacker?"

"Hell no, but at least if I was returning fire, I'd feel better." He braved another glance. "Oh, what the actual hell?"

Malcolm watched as the attacker opened a case and pulled out a bottle, the top of which was plugged with a rag.

"Damn it."

Mary looked at him with alarm. "What is it?"

"It must be happy hour, because there's going to be Molotov cocktails on the menu."

"Do we have time to rush the attacker?"

"No," Malcolm said after another quick glance. "Two handguns on their waist. We'd be dead in less than twenty feet. Incoming!"

The large, flaming bottle flew into the house through the now-broken front door, and it impacted in the entryway beside the living room. The flames ignited the quickly-spreading liquid with a loud *foom* noise, turning that section of the living room into an instant inferno. The flames hungrily devoured the fuel-soaked carpeting, and began feasting on the low-hanging drapes.

The assailant threw a second bottle up high, and both Malcolm and Mary heard it impact on the floor of the upstairs bedroom, just above their heads. A third went through the bedroom window on the main floor.

Malcolm took another quick peek around the corner. "You want the good news first, or the bad news?"

Mary glared at him. "How could there possibly be any good news right now?"

"The good news is neither of us has been shot yet." He took a quick look into the front room. "I'd be hard-pressed to find more good news than that, although we weren't looking forward to painting the living room, and in a few minutes, there won't be a living room left to paint. The bad news is the oxygen in the room is disappearing and we'll asphyxiate in a few minutes if we don't get out of here. Oh, and I see our attacker has just finished reloading, so stay where you are."

Malcolm and Mary heard another whirr from the machine gun. Their surroundings shattered, while bullets ripped through furniture and fixtures, pinging and ricocheting all around them. The flames spread farther across the living room carpet, and were now licking uncomfortably close to the two, yet neither Malcolm nor Mary could move, as the bullets continued to spray all around them. The growing flames were accompanied by billowing, black smoke, which was thickening at an exponential rate.

Malcolm peered around the corner, but as he did, the flames had found a new fuel source and sent a hot blast into the air, which scalded his right shoulder and cheek.

"Damn it." He clutched his face.

"What happened?"

"Forget it." Malcolm said through gritted teeth. "This is way beyond needing a fire extinguisher, so we have to get out of here."

"Let's crawl toward the back door."

"No, wait," Malcolm squeezed his stinging eyes shut. "Right now, this is the only cover we have that can resist bullets. It's fifteen feet to the back door, and there's nothing to protect us from gunfire along the way. I can't see the shooter through all the damned smoke."

"But that also means the shooter can't see us either."

"We also don't know if there's someone waiting out back to shoot us the second we step out there."

"We have to chance it," Mary began crawling toward the back door, but Malcolm grabbed her foot to stop her. She looked back at him. "What are you doing?"

"It's too dangerous."

Look, you're right, we *might* die out there, but we will *definitely* die if we stay in here. We have to go, and you're leaving too, so don't even think about fighting."

The shooter had switched to single-shots, and was shooting one bullet at a time, left, right, up, down, seemingly in a random order, making predictability difficult.

"You go first," Malcolm said. "I'll make sure our attacker doesn't come inside until you're safely out."

"What's your plan if they do come inside? Cough some soot on them? You're not armed. The fight's over and we lost, so there's nothing left for us to do except get out of here alive, so we can hope for a rematch. Now come on and follow me to the back door. We do this together, whether we live or die."

"Okay, you're right," Malcolm coughed. "But at least wait until they pause to reload."

Mary nodded while also coughing.

The seconds passed agonizingly slow until there was a brief pause in the shots. Malcolm and Mary crawled with haste, scrambling toward the back door. Malcolm was unable to see anything through the smoke, but he felt around for the handle of a cupboard in the kitchen island near the back door. His stinging eyes were now squeezed shut, so he opened the cupboard door and felt around inside. His hands found one of his guns and a canvas bag. He grabbed both and resumed crawling until he was outside.

The gunfire had ceased, and there were the faint sounds of sirens in the distance, getting louder as they made their way to the scene. Malcolm and Mary both lay on the grass of their small backyard, coughing. Their faces were partially blackened, most notably below their nostrils, as they'd been exhaling soot and smoke. Their clothes were singed and blackened.

Malcolm attempted to speak, but it came out as a coughing fit. His second attempt was more successful. "You okay?"

"No," Mary moaned, her throat raspy. "I'm alive and seem to have all of my extremities intact, but I'm far from okay. My eyes sting like crazy and I can't fully open them yet."

Malcolm blinked continuously and saw the orange and red flames raging out the windows, licking hungrily at the outside walls. "That's probably for the best. Hey, remember when you said the bullet-resistant window in the front room wasn't worth the money I spent on it? Well, it just saved our lives."

"You're right, it did." Mary coughed, then blinked a few times until she could catch a glimpse of their home. She saw the thick, billowing, black and grey smoke darkening the sky above their home. She coughed again. "Let's see if you're still singing its praises once we've been living under it for a few days, seeing as how it might end up being the only piece of the house that survives."

"Good point." Malcolm looked at the house, which now was completely engulfed in smoke and flames. "Okay, so *now* we have no resources."

Mary was able to keep her eyes open somewhat longer, and she blinked as she watched her home belching smoke. She looked at Malcolm. "What's wrong with me?"

"This isn't the best time for a loaded question like that."

"It's not meant to be a loaded question." Mary coughed. "Alyssa's missing, I'm watching our house burn, and some nut just tried to barbecue us, but I don't feel anything. Just adrenaline, and a bad case of the shakes."

"There's nothing wrong with you," Malcolm managed between coughs. "After decades of trauma, excitement, and near-death experiences, your body's gotten used to it all."

"That can't be healthy." Mary looked at Malcolm. "Oh my good God. We need to get you to a hospital to get those burns treated."

"I'm fine."

"You are nowhere near fine, so stop being a stubborn man and let me look at you."

Mary inspected the burns on his cheek and shoulder. "It looks like first degree burns. I won't know for sure until I can look at it without all the soot covering it. We need to cool the skin quickly, or it could blister. It's a good thing we got out of there when we did."

"It was only good because we didn't get shot. Otherwise, leaving would have been a bad idea."

"We'd be dead by now had we stayed in there any longer, so either way it was going to be bad. Leaving was the least-worst option we had." Mary looked at his burns again. "You need to get those burns looked at, and we both need to be treated for smoke inhalation."

"Yeah, but we'll treat our conditions ourselves. Right now, I don't trust anyone."

"I suppose I can't really blame you for saying that, after this." Mary made a face and pointed at the canvas bag Malcolm had brought out. "What's that?"

"It's one of the bug-out bags I had stashed around the house." He began to unzip it. "If we ever needed to leave the house in a hurry, I had some bags we could just grab and go. Each one has two bank cards in them, and I made an assortment of bags, so we'd be ready for any emergency. This bag will have everything we need for at least… aw, goddamn it."

"What?"

"Of all the bags I could have grabbed," Malcolm fumed, "I took the damned bag of leftover gear. Aside from the bank cards, it's only got a roll of *federal quarantine zone* hazard tape, the stuffed bear nanny camera, and a protective hazmat suit in it."

"Hardly my choice for a change of clothing, but if we get desperate enough, we may have to use it." She coughed again. "None of that is terribly helpful, except for the bank cards. Any idea who the shooter was?"

"If I had to bet, I'd lay all my chips on it being the same shooter who went into the law firm looking for your uncle. We'd sure as hell better find out who she is before she kills someone."

"Call it in." Mary lay on her back and closed her eyes. "We've been attacked, so they have to help us now."

"Can't." Malcolm made a face. "As much as I'd love to call them and tell them exactly what I'm thinking about them at this moment, my phone was on the dining room table, and was last seen sharing space with the flames."

Mary sighed. "I have mine. I'll call it in."

"Call while we move." Malcolm groaned as he stood up. "I want to be away from here before the cops arrive and start asking me a bunch of dumb questions."

2:32 p.m.

A few houses down the block, Malcolm stood in the dim back corner of an open carport. There was no car in the driveway, but there were some old tires, pieces of stacked lumber, and a large clay pot with a six-foot tree growing in it. Malcolm stepped out from behind the tree when Mary returned to the carport. He looked at her and she shook her head.

"Our employer said no."

Malcolm's eyes widened. "How could they *possibly* have said no to our request for help after that?"

Mary looked at her phone and frowned. "They said it's up to us to identify the threat and then confirm it was a foreign source, or verify that we were targeted because of our jobs, and that this wasn't just some random break-and-enter."

"Every time I think I've heard the stupidest damned thing possible in a day, I get proven wrong." Malcolm coughed and then glared at the blameless tree, as he had nobody else to glare at. "Who the hell do they think would begin a goddamned break and enter with a goddamned spray of bullets from a goddamned M-60 machine gun?"

Mary shrugged. "I'm just the messenger."

"I know, I know, I'm sorry." Malcolm pointed at her phone. "Did you send them a photo of our home doing its impression of *Dante's Inferno* with a caption reading *does this look like a goddamned random break and enter to you, you clueless, vacuous imbeciles?*"

"I did send them photos, but without any of your proposed captions."

"And?"

"They did help us a little bit." Mary made a sour face. "They said they had high confidence that China, Iran, and North Korea weren't involved in the attack."

"Well, I guess that's three countries off the list." Malcolm shook his head, then squatted down. "Okay, so who else have we pissed off?"

"Let me put it this way," Mary leaned her head against the wall. "That's three countries down, and somewhere around ninety-seven to go."

"Jesus, I'm suddenly regretting every decision I've ever made and every path I've taken if we've accumulated that many enemies along the way." Malcolm stood up again and began pacing. "Okay, so what's the common denominator between us and your uncle? Alyssa, for one, and any other family member for another."

"That doesn't exactly narrow it down."

"No, it doesn't." Malcolm sighed. "So that means we need to keep digging. As soon as we can confirm who is behind the attacks, we can get our employer involved, and then we'll have help and resources."

"Speaking of our employer," Mary lifted her head and faced Malcolm. "I also submitted our request for emergency accommodations. There's nothing available for at least a week, but they said we can grab a motel and they'll reimburse us for it."

"That's something, I guess." Malcolm muttered. "You know, the cops already have our entire yard taped off. Between the cops and fire department, I figure half the city's budget is on our property right now."

"We can't think about that right now. We need a place to stay and some equipment to use, so that means we urgently need money."

"Okay, I have the two emergency bank cards with me, so I'll go get some cash and find us a motel. We can stay there until they can find us a new place."

Mary looked at him. "And you're going to run these errands looking like that?"

Malcolm shrugged then winced, due to the burn on his shoulder. "What choice do I have? A bio-hazard outfit would draw even more attention than me looking like I camped out in a volcano. The owners of this lovely carport are out of town, so just lay low in here for a few minutes until I return. The bank machine is just a block away."

"Is it safe?" Mary looked worried. "How do we know that trigger-happy house-burner isn't waiting for us to show ourselves in public?"

"We don't, but I'm sure as hell not hiding in a carport all day." Malcolm winked at her. "I'll be fine. I'm just going to the bank and back."

"Fine. When you bring the cash back, I'll get some items from the drug store to patch us both up and grab a new laptop while you find us a place to stay."

"Sounds like a plan." Malcolm began to walk out of the carport. "Damn, these burns hurt like hell."

3:50 p.m.

Karl Oberman, manager and owner of the Barclay Court Motel, was about to learn a valuable life lesson. He was of the mistaken opinion he had seen it all in his twenty-plus years of running the motel, but he was about to experience something he hadn't experienced in quite some time: complete surprise.

It occurred at 3:50 that afternoon, when a disheveled man walked through the front door of the motel's office. He had seen hundreds of disheveled people over the years, but nothing quite like this particular fellow, who was covered in soot, wore clothing which seemed to alternate between singed and charred, and had some sort of burns on his right cheek and shoulder.

"Hey," Malcolm nodded to Karl.

"Holy…" Karl's mouth hung agape, and looked at Malcolm with alarm. "Are you okay, sir?"

"No, and I think that much should have been pretty damned obvious to you before you asked that question."

"What can I do to help?"

Malcolm coughed. "I need to rent a room for a week, possibly longer, and I need it now. I want a room with a double bed or bigger, a shower, and a kitchenette."

"So, just to be clear," Karl cleared his throat. "Do you really think renting a room is your biggest need right now?"

"Let's be realistic, pal." Malcolm locked eyes with him. "In terms of the needs I have which you are going to be able to help me with, yeah, I do. How about we start with the room and see how it goes?"

"I guess that's fair enough." The man began clicking and typing on the computer beside him. "Okay, room twenty-four is free. It has a queen-sized bed and it fits your needs perfectly. Will it be just yourself?"

"No, there'll be two of us." Malcolm sniffed, which caused him to cough again. "My wife will be with me."

"Is she also…?"

"If you're wondering if she also looks like a piece of toast that was thrown into a blast furnace, yeah, she does, hence why I mentioned the need for a shower in the suite."

The man made an awkward and uncomfortable face as he looked at Malcolm. "Er…"

"What?"

"Do you have some ID with you, by chance? And I'll need to know your method of payment."

Malcolm fished a card out of the pocket of his soot-covered jeans. "Here's my ID. It's a little melted around the edges, but it's still readable. Method of payment will be cash."

The man nodded and typed on his computer for a minute, though it felt like ten minutes to Malcolm.

"Thank you," the man handed Malcolm back his ID card. "I see you live just a few blocks from here. Taking a stay-cation?"

"Take a good, close look at me, pal," Malcolm pointed to his own face. "My face doesn't look like this because I got a sunburn from playing beach volleyball, so ask yourself if I look as though I'm in holiday mode. Do you often see vacationers looking as though they were standing at the epicenter of the Krakatoa eruption?"

The man winced. "Well, no, now that you mention it. I was just trying to make some chit-chat."

"Listen to me very carefully," Malcolm sighed. "I am here because I had to evacuate my home, so the fewer inane questions you ask, the happier a customer I'm going to be."

"It's just…" the motel manager struggled for the words to follow. He waved his hands in front of himself and gestured vaguely towards Malcolm. "You look… well, you look a bit *distressed*."

"Distressed?" Malcolm glared at the man. "You smell that, pal? It's smoke. My house just burned down, okay? And I spent an inadvisably long time inside of the house while it was on fire and filled with smoke because, if you can believe this, for a couple of minutes, it was the safest place I had access to. You ever sat too close to a campfire? Well multiply that by several factors of ten, and you might have an idea of what my living room felt like. You see the soot all over my face and clothes? Same reason. Big fire, house gone. See the first-degree burns on parts of my skin? That wasn't caused by me forgetting to apply sunscreen, that's from the heat of the flames from the fire that destroyed my house. Let's just say the temperature was considerably more than our air conditioner could keep up with, okay? See where my clothes got charred? Yeah, that's not the look I was going for when I got dressed this morning, that happened while I was trying to get myself out of my house, which was – as I hope I've made abundantly clear by now – on fire. So, I'd say my appearance goes several miles past *distressed,* took the off-ramp through *troubled,* hung a right at *discomposed,* drove a few blocks past *jarred,* and then parked outside the door of *needs immediate medical attention.*"

"I'm sorry to hear that."

"No, you being sorry may come later, if you don't listen to me extremely carefully right now." Malcolm's eyes narrowed and he leaned on the counter. "I've had a particularly bad day, so I want no disturbances. Not a phone call, not a wave from the window, nothing. While I'm here, I don't want to see another human being, okay? I don't even want to see housekeeping unless we specifically ask for them. If anyone employed or contracted by this motel so much as knocks on my door, I will devote the rest of my life to bringing misery and discomfort to everyone running this place. If anyone is crazy enough to set foot inside of our suite, then everyone on this entire city block will understand why I look like this, because they will end their day looking the same or considerably worse. If you have any questions, *any questions at all,* this is your one and only chance to ask them, because once I leave this office, I don't want to see you again for a week, and believe me, you sure as hell don't want to see me either. So, are there any questions?"

"None, sir. Here are your room passes, and this is your copy of the paperwork."

Malcolm looked closer at the man. "What's your name?"

"Karl. I'm the owner and manager here."

"I appreciate your help, Karl. If you follow my requests to the letter, I will be a very, very satisfied customer who owes you a favour. You don't know me, but I'm the sort of person you would really want to have owing you a favour. If you do not follow my requests, then I won't simply write a bad review, okay? The entire metro region will hear about of my displeasure through the inevitable news reports which will follow."

"I understand, sir. And you'll receive nothing from us without you asking for it."

"I like you, Karl." Malcolm gave him an appreciative nod. "I can see we're going to get along just fine."

4:21 p.m.

Newberg drove along West 33rd as he spoke on his flip phone. Browne, in the passenger seat, looked over at him as soon as the call ended. "Well?"

"We just got our first break," Newberg signalled and then turned down the next street. "I just got word from the Lieutenant that Mercer and Bristol checked into the Barclay Court Motel on East Twenty-Second Street half an hour ago."

"The Barclay?" Browne's eyebrows shot up. "Isn't that Karl's place?"

"Yes, it is." Newberg beamed. "I think I'm due to catch up with an old friend."

"Finally, something is going our way. Let's get over there now."

4:22 p.m.

There is a small duty-free store in the small border town of Blaine, Washington, near the corner of C Street and 2nd Street. Abby and Alyssa had made their way to that location after abandoning their stolen car near the border. They then crossed the border using a narrow, underground smuggling tunnel which Abby knew about from her years spent ding jobs for Marcus, as his associates occasionally used it as a mean to bring gasoline, dairy, and cigarettes into Canada, and marijuana, hemp, and alcohol back into the United States.

Once across, they emerged on A Street in Blaine, and had made their way to the duty-free store's parking lot. Technically, they were in the adjacent lot of *Big Al's Diner,* which people used for overflow parking when the store was busy but the diner was not.

Abby was inspecting a sedan, whose owners had just parked and departed, heading toward the restaurant. As Abby looked over the vehicle, Alyssa approached her.

"I take it you're checking out this car because you're thinking of stealing it."

"Yup." Abby sighed. "It would be perfect, but it has an anti-theft alarm and engine immobilizer."

"Can you bypass the alarm?"

Abby nodded. "Yes, I could get in and stop the alarm in under forty seconds, then another two to three minutes to bypass the engine immobilizer."

"Okay, then I'm waiting for the part where you leap into action and do those things."

"Then you'll have to keep waiting, because I can't *leap into action* without my tools, equipment, and software." Abby slouched. "I'm really not as prepared for this as I thought I was. I'm only now realizing how much I depended on Ryan."

"Ryan?" Alyssa thought for a moment. "I just thought he was the bouncer and bartender at Marcus' bar. I didn't know he was involved in your…. Extracurricular activities."

"It was his also his job to keep me organized, and he always made sure I brought what I needed to each job and it's made me realize that without my stuff, I'm completely useless."

"No, that's not true at all. You're amazing and a lot more capable than you think you are." Alyssa hugged Abby. "Even without tools, you're still way more competent at this sort of thing than I'd ever be."

"Thanks." Abby blushed. "I wish my brain let me organize things better. I'm really good at reacting in the *right now,* but I'm terrible at anticipating what I might need tomorrow."

"I'm the opposite. I worry all the time, so I tend to over-prepare for what I might need tomorrow, but I rarely have a clue about what to do *right now.*" Alyssa looked at Abby. "It would appear we have complementary skill sets."

"It's like me and my semi-sister," Abby looked at the vehicle and made a face. "We have, like, a functioning brain between us, but neither of us function well alone."

"Let's just keep walking," Alyssa tried to look positive. "We'll find a way to get to where we're going."

Abby pointed to the parking lot. "Like that bus."

Alyssa looked toward where Abby was pointing. "It says it's for hire. How about we hire the bus instead of trying to steal a ride?"

"It's worth a shot," Abby sighed. "Though not anywhere near as much fun."

4:28 p.m.

Malcolm stepped out of the motel room's bathroom and was toweling his hair. He walked toward Mary, who was sitting up on the queen-sized bed, her laptop and cables strewn around her.

"That shower sure helped," Malcolm nodded toward the new laptop. "What are you doing?"

"I connected to our employer's portal, signed in and authenticated my ID, and accessed my backup directory to where my backups live. Right now, I'm downloading the software I'll need so I can install it all."

"How's it all going?"

"All things considered, it's going well, but when I'm anxious to get working so I can try and find Alyssa, it's going torturously slow." Mary gave him a tired smile. "Still, the laptop is almost ready to go. The rest of my backup and software should be installed in about an hour, at which point I can get back to work searching for Alyssa. How are you doing?"

"I'm still coughing up soot, but not as much now. I'm just glad you were able to get us a change of clothes."

"We'll have to get some more at some point, but for now, it's the least of our priorities." She patted the space on the bed beside her. "Come over here and I'll put some fresh cream on those burns."

"What is that stuff?" he said as he sat down. "It's really been helping with the pain."

She reached over to the bedside table and opened the lid off of the plastic container. She scooped some of the translucent, off-white cream onto her fingertips. "It's mostly aluminum potassium sulfate, camphor oil, lanolin, and mineral oil."

She applied the cream to the right side of his face, being as gentle as she could. It still stung, and Malcolm winced. "Jesus, and you managed to find all those ingredients so quickly?"

Mary nodded, not taking her eyes off of what she was doing. "Between the drug store and the herbalist down the block, yes. Now hold still."

"We should talk about what our next steps are."

Mary reloaded her fingers with more of her homemade cream, then gently applied it to Malcolm's shoulder. "Once I get my software and backups loaded, I'll start using data analytics to see if I can plot a path where Alyssa is most likely to be, based on her last known location and then employing probability theory."

Malcolm winced again as Mary gingerly massaged the cream into his reddened skin. "What do you want me to do while you're doing that?"

"We're going to need more money." Mary paused to add more cream to her fingers. "I need you to go to the bank and make another withdrawal."

"Yeah, sure. That's it? Just get some money?"

"The initial money you gave me is all gone." She put the lid on the cream and placed the container on the bedside table, beside a piece of paper. "Between the first aid, the clothes, and this laptop, it didn't take long to disappear. I can't get anything else until we get some more cash."

Malcolm stood up. "Once I get more money, what else do you need?"

"I wrote out a list." Mary pointed toward the piece of paper beside the cream container. "I wrote an address at the top of that page. Take the list to that location, then hand it to Gurpreet, my tech guru. She'll supply you with everything, and we have an account there."

"We do?" Malcolm picked up the list and blinked at the many words he didn't understand. "I don't even know what any of this stuff is. I'm not looking to get out of a task, here, but this is more your ballpark than mine."

"You have no clue how to get my laptop software installed, and if there's a connection problem, you won't know how to fix it." Mary looked at him. "However, taking a list to Gurpreet, letting her compile the items, and then bringing it back is well within your capabilities."

"Good point. And you said we have an account there?"

"Yes, so expense whatever you can, and then use cash for the rest."

"Okay." Malcolm nodded. "How far is it?"

"From here, it's two blocks north, then three blocks east, but you'll need a taxi or ride-share to get it all back here."

"Fine," Malcolm exhaled. "So, how much money will I need to take out of the bank?"

"Only five thousand."

"Only?"

Mary cast a weary look at him. "I'm not exactly doing high school homework on this laptop, I'm running a lot of high-end software and I need high-end accessories so it doesn't take me all day to get results. The faster I can work, the faster we'll track down Alyssa, so I need the best accessories money can buy."

"Got it." Malcolm looked at the list again. "Can we afford all this stuff?"

"No, so that reminds me," Mary waved her finger at the list. "Keep every receipt, so we can get reimbursed for it all later."

Malcolm nodded, then finished getting dressed.

5:46 p.m.

Detectives Newberg and Browne sat in their unmarked police car. Browne, who was less than delighted with what his wife considered to be proper snack food, had given his small bag of dried fruit and nuts to his partner Newberg, who was chewing as he watched Malcolm leave the motel and descend the stairs.

"There goes Mercer." Newberg lowered his binoculars.

Browne nodded. "Yeah, but is Bristol in there?"

"No idea, but I know who we can ask." Newberg opened his car door once Malcolm was out of sight. "Come on."

The two men exited the vehicle and strode toward the motel's office, which was at the front of the building. As they opened the front door, an electronic chime sounded. Newberg approached the man behind the counter. "Hello Karl."

Karl suppressed his scowl and instead nodded at him. "Hey, Richie. It's good to see you. Well, *good* might be pushing it a bit. And Browne is with you, so I take it this is a business call, right?"

"I'm afraid so, but I will come by soon. It's your turn to buy the beer."

"Yeah, sure, and one day when I'm not broke, I'll consider agreeing that's even close to being accurate. So, what can I do for you?"

Newberg rested his folded arms on the counter. "We need access to one of your rooms."

"That shouldn't be too big a problem." Karl rubbed his hands together. "Which room?"

"Room twenty-four."

"Oh," Karl made a sour face and then looked at his feet. "I see."

"Is there a problem?"

"Yes, a bit of one." Karl sucked the air through his teeth, then looked up at Newberg. "You see, the thing is…"

"What?"

"The thing is, I think the guests in that room might have stepped out."

"That's what we were hoping." Newberg said in a slow, deliberate voice. "You see, we didn't *want* them to be in their room. We wanted to take a quick peek inside their room while they weren't around to object. We won't touch or remove anything, and nobody will even know we were in there."

"Look, fellas," Karl clasped his hands together and exhaled sharply. "I'm sorry, but I can't give you access."

Newberg blinked. "Seriously, Karl? How long have we been friends?"

"I've *known you* for twenty years, give or take, but I'd hardly call us—"

"It's been *twenty-two* years, Karl," Newberg interjected. "We became friends when you started dating my sister."

"Who ended up divorcing me four years ago," Karl folded his arms. "And do I need to remind you that she took every cent I had in the settlement?"

"That's not the point here. The point is we're friends, and friends should help one another."

"Since when have you helped me?"

"Karl, come on," Newberg put his hands on his hips. "I helped you with that *Drunk and Disorderly* charge you got three Christmases ago. Don't you remember me making that go away for you?"

"Yes," Karl frowned, "and in return you got me to buy pizza for the entire day shift at your precinct. It would have been cheaper for me to have paid the fine."

"And last month," Newberg pressed on, undeterred, "I took care of that drunk guy in your parking lot who was mooning everyone, and it wasn't even my job to do that."

Karl rolled his eyes. "The drunk guy was your nephew, and you're the one who got him drunk in the first place."

"The point is, I helped you." Newberg nodded. "Aside from the pizza thing, which I admit was a mistake, I have *never* asked you for anything in return, have I?"

Karl looked miserable. "Well, no, pizza aside, I suppose you haven't."

Newberg shook his head, in an exaggerated manner. "And now that I need one little favour from you…"

"Listen, Richie," Karl wiped the newly-formed perspiration from his brow as he recalled the alarming warnings he'd received earlier from a half-crazed, soot-covered man with skin burns. "Even if I did *sort of* owe you, it can't be room twenty-four. If it was any other room, I would."

Browne folded his arms. "What's so special about that room?"

"The room isn't special at all," Karl swallowed. "The guests are."

Newberg turned to face Browne. "We're special too, aren't we?"

Browne looked at Newberg. "Last time I checked, yes."

"You know what else would be *special?*" Newberg raised a finger and wagged it. "We could arrange for a *special* health inspection of these *special* premises."

"Or," Browne added with mock excitement, "we could get a *special* court order and shut down the entire motel while we conduct a *special* investigation."

"Oh, hey," Newberg snapped his fingers. "What about a *special* raid of every occupied room, if we were to come up with a *special* kind of probable cause?"

Browne nodded. "That would really be *special.*"

"It would be *very* special." Newberg turned to face Karl. "Doesn't that sound like fun, Karl?"

"No," he sighed. "I'd prefer to avoid anything special."

"Of course you would," Newberg smiled. "So, you need to weigh, on one side, upsetting two special guests, versus on the other side, upsetting all your other guests, upsetting us, upsetting a health inspector, and upsetting your lawyer, who will need to help you navigate through an unnecessarily complicated court order. Now, which side of the scale do you think has the bigger set of problems for you?"

Browne chimed in when the silence had gone on for considerably longer than he had expected it to. "Well?"

Karl wiped his forehead again. "I'm still deciding."

"Oh, hey, Karl, I almost forgot." Browne stroked his chin as though deep in thought. "Your fiancé, who works here as a housekeeper... didn't her work permit recently expire?"

Karl closed his eyes and exhaled. "I'll take you to room twenty-four."

"Thanks, Karl." Newberg feigned a look of surprise. "My heavens, your cooperation has made me completely forget what it was we were just talking about."

Browne aped the same expression. "I've forgotten, too."

"Now," Newberg folded his arms. "Which way is room twenty-four?"

Karl waved his hand. "Follow me."

5:50 a.m.

Newberg looked over at Karl, who was standing more than ten feet away and refusing to come any closer to the room. "Are you sure this is the right key card?"

"Yes, it's a master key," Karl pointed at it. "It should open every door here."

"Well, it's not working. Come and see for yourself."

"I'd rather not get any closer to their door than I already am, if it's all the same to you."

"Do you want to come here and take a look," Newberg snapped, "or do you want to have to explain to your fiancé why getting a new visa is suddenly so difficult, and why Immigration officials are wanting to ask her a lot of questions?"

"Alright, alright." Karl inched his way toward the door, until he was just able to clearly see the card reader on the door handle. "Wait a minute." He frowned. "Oh, that is *completely* against motel policy."

"What is?"

"It looks as though they've changed the lock."

Newberg nodded. "Then it looks to me like we have the *probable cause* we were looking for."

"I concur."

"Okay, stand back while I kick in the door."

Karl retreated with haste back to his ten-foot distance while Newberg stomped his foot into the door beside the handle. The door didn't budge and Newberg wrapped his arms around his newly-injured leg, while hopping up and down on his other. After a few seconds, he lowered his leg and limped toward Karl.

"Don't just stand there with your mouth hanging open, Karl. Go back to your office and bring me a sledgehammer."

"I don't have one. This may come as a surprise to you, Richie, but it's hardly an item guests routinely ask me for."

"Never mind, I've got one in the truck of our car. I'll go and get it."

Before Newberg could turn to leave, the motel room door opened and Mary stood at the doorway looking at the two men. "Oh, hello again detectives. What are you doing here?"

"I am so sorry about this, ma'am," Karl called out from his safe distance while looking wretched. "I swear this wasn't my idea. I thought you were out."

"What he means," Newberg said after glaring at Karl, "was we wanted to talk to you, but we weren't sure if you were here."

"My husband stepped out, but I'm still here."

"Why did you book yourself into a motel?" Browne gestured toward the room, "Taking a local vacation or something?"

"No, our house was damaged during a break-in, so we're staying here for now."

"I'm sorry, I had no idea." Browne pulled out his smartphone. "Do you know which officer was assigned to the case? I will personally call them and make sure it's treated as a high priority."

"We haven't reported the break-in to the local police. We've instead alerted the appropriate *federal* authorities."

"Wait a minute." Browne tapped a few buttons on his phone and scrolled down, scanning the screen for what he was looking for. "I saw an alert about an incident on 29th Avenue. Was it your house that was attacked earlier today?"

"Unfortunately, yes."

"I should have known." Newberg looked over Browne's arm and read the summary of what took place. "Of course it would be your house where something like that happened."

He read some more, while shaking his head. "This is what's left of your house." Newberg raised his eyebrows and turned Browne's phone to face Mary so she could see the picture. "You see that? Are you seriously choosing to describe what happened there as a break in?"

Mary shrugged. "There was definitely breakage, our security was compromised, and we experienced material losses, so it ticks the three essential boxes."

Newberg handed the phone back to Browne, still staring at the screen. "You know, most break-ins don't result in this many shell casings on the street."

"Close to *two hundred* shell casings, to be a bit more precise." Browne scrolled through the report on his screen, shaking his head. "A typical break-in also rarely results in that much fire, smoke, and debris. I mean, I'm looking at this more recent picture of what used to be your house, and your three-story home is less than one-story now. Your front pathway appears to meet up with what looks to have been an upstairs bedroom window, and your main floor is now sharing space with your basement."

Mary rubbed her eyes. "So far, all you've done is tell me the things I already know. Can you switch it up, and get to whatever it is you want to ask me?"

"Unbelievable." Newberg shook his head slowly. "Wherever you go, disasters happen, and you just seem to shrug it off as though it happens every day. Did the property values in this neighbourhood suddenly plummet when you first moved in?"

"My daughter is missing, so I don't have time for your asinine questions."

"Okay, then how about this question instead. When was the last time you saw your daughter?"

"Not since she left for work." Mary glared at him. "You know, on that day when you arrested her and then lost her while she was supposedly in your custody."

"So, she's not there in the room with you right now?"

"No, we don't know where she is, and I'm worried about her. So, if you're done, I'd like to get back to trying to track her down."

"No, I'm not done. I'm nowhere even close to being done. We need to take a look inside your suite."

"Sure," Mary nodded, "but first let me see your warrant."

"We don't need a warrant when we have probable cause."

"Based on what?"

"You changed the locks," Newberg said as he tapped his finger on the new card reader on the door. "That violates your contract with the motel, and it certainly qualifies as suspicious behaviour to me."

"We didn't violate the contract at all. Under section five of the agreement my husband signed, under the subsection titled *damages,* it states we are not to damage anything, which we haven't, and subsection 5c states we are not to make any permanent alterations. This lock is temporary, and we'll put it back to how it was before we arrived. Well, not quite, actually, it will be *better* than it was. The card-access locking mechanism was sticking, which is why my husband removed it in the first place. He's oiled and greased the mechanisms, and he'll put it back on once he's finished repairing it."

Karl called out from the distance. "Oh, thank you very kindly."

In a perfectly synchronized motion, both detectives turned and glared at Karl, then turned back to face Mary.

"Okay, fine." Newberg wagged his finger at Mary. "But this stalling won't buy you as much time as you're hoping it will. We'll be back in a matter of minutes with that warrant."

Mary watched the two detectives turn away, after flashing a look of annoyance at her. They began descending the stairs. When they were nearly at the bottom, Karl shuffled over to Mary and leaned in so he could whisper to her. "You can keep the bathroom towels if you don't tell your husband I was here, okay?"

"Got it," she winked.

Mary closed the door, locked it, and then sighed. The detectives were yet another complication and distraction she didn't need or have time for. How could she get some peace and quiet so she could focus on what she needed to do?

A thought occurred to her, and she went over to the canvas bag Malcolm had brought from the house. She unzipped it and looked at the contents.

"Huh. Maybe this bag of stuff is going to come in handy after all." She looked around the room. "I'd better get packing."

5:52 p.m.

Alyssa's eyes scanned the small town, taking in the buildings and businesses within her line of sight.

Abby looked at her. "You ever been to Baneridge before?"

"No, never. I think my parents mentioned the name to me at one point, but this is my first time seeing it."

"There's not much here, but it was home for me a few years back."

"You're from Baneridge?"

"No, but it was where I lived for quite a long time."

Alyssa glanced at her. "Can I see where you used to live?"

"That's where we're going, but before I take you there, I need you to swear upon your life that you won't tell anyone what you see once you're there."

Alyssa's face wrinkled in confusion. "Why?"

Abby sighed. "Just swear to me you'll keep what you see secret and I'll explain."

"Okay, I swear to you my secrecy. But why? What's so special about your old house?"

"I didn't live in a house." Abby pointed down the street at a three-story building. "I lived in that hospital, and my biggest secret is in there."

5:54 p.m.

"What the hell is this?" Newberg looked at the yellow and black hazard tape criss-crossing the door frame of room twenty-four. The tape was imprinted with the words *Danger Biohazard Zone.* "Is she kidding with this?"

There was a notice attached to the door. A half-page of text was printed on it, and Browne leaned in to read it.

Newberg held up his hands. "What does it say?"

"It says *danger.*" Browne shrugged and kept reading. *"Biohazard area. This area is now sealed due to a suspected chemical spill."*

"Chemical spill?"

Browne shrugged again and continued reading. *"Federal authorities have been notified and will respond as per applicable emergency response legislation. No entry under penalty of applicable federal laws* and then it cites a piece of legislation. Is this notice for real?" Browne took out his smartphone and did a quick search. He nodded. "It cites the correct federal statutes for a biohazard incident."

Newberg wagged his finger at the door. "That notice wasn't there twenty minutes ago."

"Who are these people?" Browne scratched his head then pointed to the notice. "This is not normal."

"No, this isn't anything even close to normal." Newberg growled. "To hell with this. We're going in anyway. We've got a warrant."

"Hold up a second," Browne held up his hand. "The warrant we have is useless now, and you know it. Federal disaster laws supersede local authority. The second that notice was taped to the door, it became a federal matter, putting it out of our jurisdiction."

"I don't care at this point. I'm going in no matter what the piece of paper says."

"You're going to illegally trespass into a federally-mandated biohazard zone?"

"It's not a real biohazard, idiot, use your head." Newberg poked at the air in front of the door. "They're trying to jerk us around again, but I'm through playing by their rules on this one. We need to know what they're hiding and what they're up to, and we're always going to be a step behind them if we go completely by the book."

Browne clucked his tongue. "I don't know."

"Look, they may be running interference in our investigation, which is a sort of obstruction of justice. We need to end that now."

"We might be able to make the obstruction angle stick, but it all goes out the window if the room is registered as a biohazard."

"It's not." Newberg fumed. "There's no way."

"Okay, so how do we get inside?"

"The window. We can pop out this moulding, remove the pane of glass, and then climb in."

Newberg pulled out a pocketknife and slid it along the narrow gap where the weathered aluminum strip pressed against the pane of glass. The decades-old adhesive holding the strip in place offered little resistance. The three remaining strips relented just as easily, and then with great care, the two detectives lowered the plane of glass down and leaned it with great care against the wall.

Newberg stood up, pushed aside the curtain, and then climbed inside the room, peppering his efforts with grunts and a series of groans. Once Newberg was inside, Browne followed, with considerably less effort. Browne quickly scanned the room. "It looks empty."

"No, no, it can't be." Newberg stomped around the room. "Check under the bed, in the closet, everywhere. Why would they go through all this trouble to keep us out if there's nothing inside the room to see? Look everywhere, just in case, and be sure to look for any evidence their daughter was here."

Browne pointed at an object on top of the clothes bureau. "Such as a stuffed bear?"

Newberg walked over to Browne and looked at it. "Yeah, a stuffed bear is exactly the sort of thing I was talking about. But why is it still here? Why didn't they take it with them?"

"They must have wanted us to find it."

"Give Detective Browne a prize," the stuffed bear said. More specifically, Mary's voice came through a speaker which was implanted *inside* the stuffed bear. "We need to have a little talk."

"I agree," Newberg snapped. "And it'll be a talk about what constitutes *obstruction of justice* laws."

"At best, your obstruction allegations are based on circumstantial evidence and your own guesswork, whereas I have video proof of you two defying a federal quarantine." Mary continued. "That's a felony, as I'm sure you know, and it comes with a mandatory prison sentence of no less than six months."

Newberg seethed. "The quarantine isn't real."

"It is real. Check your phone, Detective Browne. I just sent a copy of the federal confirmation to each of you."

Newberg looked over and read the message as Browne did the same. Newberg looked at the bear, fuming. "How the hell did you do all that in twenty minutes?"

"My efficiency is the least of your problems at the moment," Mary continued. "You will both lose your badges over this, and I wonder how your fellow inmates will react when they find out you're disgraced cops. In short, your careers are over. Unless, of course…"

"Unless, huh?" Newberg snapped. "Yeah, I saw this part coming five miles away. This is the part where you shake us down or try to blackmail us."

"I prefer the term *incentivise*."

"Yeah? We'll see how *incentivised* we are in a minute." Newberg put his hands on his hips. "What exactly do you want?"

"Just twenty minutes of your time. Are you willing to sit down and listen to what we've found with an open mind?"

"That's it?" Newberg looked at the bear with suspicion. "You mean if we listen to you, all of this goes away?"

"If you listen really well, then yes, it will go away and the recordings I have will be deleted. But if you've truly listened, then I imagine you'll be far more interested in acting on the information I give you."

"Then let's meet."

"I'll set something up soon. I just need a couple more puzzle pieces and then I'll have what I need to convince you. For the sake of your careers, though, stay away from my husband and I until you hear from me. I'm on my way back to the motel, and I'd suggest you not be there by the time I arrive, which means you'd better fix that window quickly."

5:59 p.m.

Just outside of the hospital's main entrance, Alyssa turned to face Abby. "There's a guard at the front desk, and everyone is showing him ID cards as they enter. We won't get past him without one."

"Then we're perfectly fine, because I have a fake ID card already made up for you."

Alyssa took the card and stared at it. "This is amazing. If you hadn't told me it was fake, I would never have guessed it."

"Meh." Abby wrinkled her nose. "Sure, I mean, it looks good and all, but it'll be useless once you get inside. Like, it won't open any doors or anything, it'll just get you past the guard."

"What about you?"

"Don't worry. I have a pass, too."

"Okay, good." Alyssa nodded. "So what's our plan?"

"That depends." Abby looked at her. "How good are you at pretending?"

"I pretend to come from a normal family all the time, so I think I'm good enough at it. Why?"

"Listen closely. Once we go inside, you have to pretend my name is Katherine. Can you do that?"

"Katherine?" Alyssa squinted and her brow furrowed. "Okay, but why?"

"Long story, no time right now. I also need you to pretend you took me out for a walk, and we left through the east entrance."

"I'm going to have so many questions about this later."

"Repeat it back to me."

"Your name is Katherine, I took you for a walk, and we left through the east entrance."

"Good." Abby beamed. "And then tell me, in front of the guard, that it's time for me to go back to my room."

"Um… okay."

The two stepped through the front door hospital and the guard at the desk glanced at their badges. He then saw Abby and smiled at her. "Hey, Kat. Did you have a nice walk?"

"Yes." Abby looked at him, glassy-eyed. "We saw a butterfly, and some pretty yellow flowers."

"That's nice." The guard at the desk squinted at his clipboard then looked up at Alyssa. "Hey, uh, Kat wasn't signed out."

"Oh," Alyssa said with a nod. "Yes, sorry. I took her out through the east entrance."

The guard made a note on the sign-in sheet. "Okay, but from now on, only take her out through this exit, understand? We need to keep records of everyone's comings and goings."

"You're right, and I will from now on, sorry." Alyssa cleared her throat. "Come on, Katherine. It's time to go back to your room."

They walked past the desk and Abby guided Alyssa around the corner, and the two proceeded down a long corridor. The hallway was busy with hospital staff moving about and going from task to task. No-one gave Abby and Alyssa so much as a glance.

Alyssa looked at Abby. "Were you, like, a patient in this facility?"

"Yeah." Abby then hummed and hawed. "And I think I technically still am."

"Except here, your name is Katherine?"

"No," Abby shook her head. "Katherine's name is Katherine; I just look identical to her. No-one except Ramona can tell who's who, so that's how I can come and go from here as I please."

"You've mentioned Ramona to me before, but who's… oh wait." Alyssa snapped her fingers. "Katherine. You mentioned someone named *Kat* to me when we first met. You referred to her as your semi-sister. Is that who you're referring to?"

"Yup. She's my sister from the same mister, and my *other* from another mother."

"Oh, then I'd love to meet her." Alyssa's face brightened. "Will you introduce me to her?"

Abby pondered Alyssa's words before replying. "From what I understand, I don't know if it's possible."

"Why not?"

"That's also a long story, and again, there's no time." Abby pointed to a solid metal door a few metres ahead of them. "Just up ahead there is the secure door to the basement."

"But you said my access card is fake, so it won't open it."

"I know," Abby nodded, "but my card will open every door in this building."

"You were a patient here, yet you have an access card to the entire hospital?"

"Yeah, that's what I just told you."

Alyssa exhaled, sharply. "The lunatics have truly taken over the asylum."

"Who better to look after our needs than ourselves?" Abby grinned. "And the basement isn't really an asylum, it's more like... *protective custody*. The basement is for highly unusual or gifted patients who don't want to spend their lives as rats in a lab. Oh, and if anyone asks who you are, tell them you're with *Special Projects* on level three."

"What if someone asks me something medical or technical?"

"They won't." Abby placed her pass in front of the card reader and the door unlocked. "Those of us who live in the basement *are* the special projects, and nobody knows much about the day-to-day operations down there except for a few people on the third floor." Abby pulled the door open and gestured for Alyssa to go through. "Most of the regular staff here are too overworked and too tired to care about what anyone else is doing, anyway."

Alyssa stepped in and waited for Abby to follow. "And if someone who is actually part of Special Projects approaches me? What then?"

"If that happens," Abby pulled the door closed behind her, "then you're totally screwed, so you might as well not worry about it."

Alyssa groaned. "Why do I keep asking you for reassurances? It never works out the way I want it to."

10:16 p.m.

Antonio Bellantoni had the brim of his hat pulled down and the collar of his light jacket turned up as he walked through the back streets and alleys in the downtown core. His Uncle Sal had told him to stay in the loft until further notice, but Antonio needed to have *some* time out or he'd go stir crazy. His fiancé had been texting him, so he decided to risk a discreet rendezvous with her, just as he had done the previous night. He was on his way back to the loft, a mere five blocks away, and he made a point of the taking the backstreets and alleys to avoid being seen.

Last night had gone smoothly, but tonight he was feeling nervous. He had the feeling he was being followed, but he could neither see nor hear anything or anyone around him. He tried to dismiss his feelings as nerves, stress, or fatigue, but the sensation remained and he found it unsettling.

As he walked past an alley dumpster, a black-clad figure leapt out, wrapped an arm around his neck and used the other hand to cover his mouth. He was then spun around and taken face-down to the pavement. His attacker had him pinned to the ground, with a knee pressed firmly between his shoulder blades.

"Take my money," Antonio spoke in a rapid manner. "Take whatever you want, but please let me live."

"I'm not here to rob you," the assailant removed their black stocking mask. "Think of this instead as an unorthodox family reunion."

Antonio was able to strain his head enough that he could see his attacker. "Mary Bristol?"

"Perfect. You got it in one."

Antonio regained his composure, which was difficult to do with his face resting against alley concrete, and he huffed. "What is the meaning of this unprovoked assault? I could have you thrown in jail, and don't think I wouldn't do it."

"You're not the brightest bulb on the family Christmas tree, are you?" Mary put more weight on her knee, and Antonio grimaced. "Considering your immediate situation, I'd have hoped you'd have opted for a rational discussion based on mutual respect. I really am sorry about the measures I had to employ in order to meet with you, but Uncle Sal was going out of his way to keep us from talking, and we really do need to catch up. Here's what's going to happen. I'm going to ask you a few questions, and if you answer them, then this unpleasantness can be done with quickly. If you don't, then I'm going to inflict some harm upon you, based on a sliding scale that'll be entirely determined by my level of frustration with you at any given moment."

"You can ask whatever you wish, but I won't be telling you anything pertaining to the case. Uncle Sal told me not to speak with anyone but him." He attempted a menacing glance, but with his face turned, he more resembled a confused salmon after hitting a dam. "And now I understand why he mentioned you specifically by name. I'm going to sue you into oblivion, you know."

"That's another incredibly idiotic thing to say. You don't learn well, do you? May I remind you that you're face down in an alley, and the person you're threatening is in a position to cause you a wide array of pain?" Mary pulled his right arm behind his back and yanked it hard. "Do you think this is some stupid game, where you can cajole or threaten litigation in order to get your way? You're supposed to be the brain amongst the cousins, which is getting sadder the longer I think about it, so use your head and process your situation for a moment. In fact, I'll help you process it, so we can move this along more quickly. I've taken some notably drastic measures in order to speak with you, so assuming you have an IQ greater than a lobotomized sloth, you must be aware by now that if things have gotten to this point, then we're way beyond things being handled in a civilized way. If my asking you questions is going to result in consequences for me, then I'm going to make sure it's worth it by doing extra harm to you every time you don't cooperate."

Antonio grunted.

"In case the logical conclusion has eluded you," Mary continued, "let me spell it out. I only tracked you down once I made peace with knowing I'd be inflicting an assortment of injuries upon you, ranging from superficial to permanent, and consequences be darned."

"I don't believe any of that for a second." Antonio grunted again. "Uncle Sal would be furious, so there's no way you would risk his wrath, and no way you'd defy him. And even if you did defy him, I wouldn't. Frankly, everyone in the family will side with Uncle Sal over you, so it's both contemptible and disgraceful that you are attempting to coerce me into going against him like this."

"Mother of God, you're a dimwit." Mary gave his arm another push. "You somehow still seem unaware of how far I'll go and how little I care about what the family thinks. I've been the family outcast before, and if that's what it takes for me to get information from you, then I'll gladly be the family outcast again. And speaking of casts, you have about five seconds to change your mind about answering my questions before you start needing some casts of your own. Starting with this arm, with a break right at the elbow."

"Ow, no wait, wait. Just for the sake of my own curiosity, what *exactly* do you want to ask me about?"

"I need to know a few details about the trial." Mary tightened her grip on his forearm. "Specifically, I learned you were in the judge's chambers at the time of the blast. Why were you in there? What was the meeting about?"

"But I can't disclose that to you; it's attorney-client privilege, and I could get disbarred."

"You're unlikely to get *disbarred,* but your right shoulder is highly likely to get *dislocated.* You're right-handed, so that's really going to be a terrible inconvenience." Mary pulled his right arm further up his back until Antonio yelped. "Ever try to brush your teeth with your non-dominant hand? You might actually get good at it by the time you heal."

"Go to hell, cousin."

"I will if I have to." Mary applied more pressure. "You know, getting dressed can be quite difficult using just one functioning arm, and the real fun begins when you need to use the bathroom."

Come on, she thought. *Stop resisting. Give me something,* anything, *so I don't have to go through with this.*

Mary had convinced herself she would be able to cross the line when the time came. She had always forbidden herself from inflicting harm upon another person, unless she was being attacked or threatened. This was new ground for her, but she justified it in her head by framing it as her only hope in finding Alyssa. But now that she was here…

I can't go through with this.

Mary's eyes began to water as she felt the rush of suppressed guilt wash over her. She'd have to find another way to find her daughter, and she fought to keep any further emotions from coming to the surface. Her violent threats had turned out to be nothing more than a bluff, and her gamble had failed. How could she extricate herself from this new mess she had created for herself?

An idea popped into her head. It was a final gambit – an aptly-named *Hail Mary*.

"Now that I think about it," Mary let his arm slacken an inch or two, "you *are* family, so I suppose I should give you one final chance to answer my questions, out of respect and courtesy. Your answers can be entirely off the record, if that helps."

Antonio whimpered. "Do you *swear* none of this will come back to me?"

"I can't promise that, because it's not completely within my control, but I *can* promise you this. If anyone does hear about anything you say to me, it won't be because I blabbed. Anything you tell me will stay between you, my husband, and me, plus it will have the added bonus of allowing you to avoid any time in the hospital, which means less time for me in the Confessional."

"Okay, okay." Antonio groaned. "Listen, I needed to meet with the judge. Crown Counsel had offered a plea deal for Zanikker and the judge needed to approve it."

"What kind of deal was he being offered?"

"Zanikker handled the books for some particularly disreputable people, including a handful of folks the police had tried to arrest in the past, but always lacked the critical evidence they needed to make the charges stick. I was approached by the Crown's lead counsel and he offered a deal for me to present to Zanikker."

"And what was the deal?"

"Zanikker would turn over his books, client list, and supporting documents to the Crown, in return for his sentence being reduced to a modest fine and a hundred hours of community service. They'd told Zanikker on day one they would be trying to work out a plea deal for him."

Mary scoffed. "They were going to let that racist scumball off the hook after everything he did?"

"Look at the big picture, cousin. Zanikker's a terrible person, no question, but he's just a puny goldfish swimming in an ocean of criminals, but his information could land the cops a number of really big fish, so they're the ones who pushed for the deal."

"Did Zanikker agree to it?"

"Yes, he read the deal the same morning he was killed." Antonio groaned. "I was up until two in the morning the night before reviewing the deal to make sure every clause was airtight. An hour before the trial resumed that day, he read it and signed it right there, on the spot. I'd have been killed in the courtroom along with them, if I hadn't been in the judge's chambers with the prosecution going over the details of the plea deal."

Mary further loosened her grip. "What did the judge think?"

"She thought the deal was acceptable, and the bomb literally exploded just as she was signing it."

"So, it's possible somebody on that client list may have heard about the deal – somehow – and acted to ensure they'd remain anonymous." Mary stared at the back of Antonio's head. "Who else in your office knew about the deal?"

"Nobody, as far as I know. I'm the lead counsel, so I'm the one opposing counsel phoned in the early evening with the proposal. The two of us sent documents back and forth over secure email, but I was the only one on the defence team who knew what was happening. I was going to update my team as soon as the judge signed off."

"If you only knew about this since the evening before, then it wouldn't be enough time for anyone on Zanikker's legal team to plan an elaborate bomb attack. The plastic explosives, the timing, and materials… nothing about the bombing seems like it was a last minute improvisation."

"Can you let go of my arm, now?"

"Oh, I'm so sorry." Mary released her grip. "So, the deal came too soon for the bombing to have involved your legal team or the judge, but who else could have known about the deal?"

"I don't know, but off the top of my head, perhaps somebody in the Crown's office leaked that a plea deal was being put forward? I really don't know, seriously."

"If they told Zanikker on day one a plea deal was likely, then that would have given any number of people more than enough time to plan an attack."

"Listen, cousin, I've told you what I know."

"Yes, you have." Mary stood up. "I don't care if you try to sue me after this. The information you've given me just might save my daughter."

"Your daughter?" Antonio pulled himself up into a kneeling position. "Alyssa's in trouble?"

"Yes. Didn't you know?"

"No, this is the first I'm hearing about this." He glared at her. "You know, you should have led with that."

"I'm so very sorry." Mary winced. "Look, I'll pay for your dry cleaning, massage therapy, and whatever treatments you need because of this."

"Yes, you will, but never mind that right now. What happened to Alyssa?"

Mary summarized the events of the last two days. She wiped her eyes and sighed. "To say the least, I'm worried sick about her."

"I can only imagine, cousin." His expression softened. "Is there anything else I can do to help?"

"Actually, yes, there is one more thing, if you're willing." Mary held out her hand and she pulled him up to his feet. "I'll need you to give me Mr. Zanikker's address."

11:44 p.m.

"I suppose I shouldn't be surprised," Malcolm sighed as he scanned the mess in the apartment. "Obviously, we're not the only ones who thought there might be answers in Zanikker's humble home."

Malcolm and Mary had arrived at Zanikker's residence, a modest one-bedroom apartment in the dually misnamed *Mount Pleasant* neighbourhood in Vancouver. Mary didn't need to pick the lock because the door, although shut, hadn't been locked by the last person who had been there.

Inside the apartment, the furniture had been upended, cupboards and drawers had been opened and their contents strewn about on every surface, whether floor, countertop, or table.

In the bedroom, the mattress was leaning against the wall and had been sliced open in three places. Clothes were tossed onto the floor, and a two-drawer filing cabinet was laying on its side. It was empty, but there were stacks of papers and file folders all around it.

Malcolm whistled as he glanced up at Mary. "I'm guessing whoever did the redecorating was looking for Zanikker's books."

"Definitely," Mary squatted down and began looking through the papers on the bedroom floor. "The question is whether or not they found them in this mess."

"I'd wager they didn't."

She looked at him. "Based on what?"

"The mess itself." Malcolm waved his hands at the scattered debris. "There's signs of a methodical search, but there's other stuff which was just thrown around, as though out of frustration. I don't know for sure, but my bet is that at least the second person left here disappointed."

"The *second* person?"

Malcolm scanned the floor. "Yeah, no one searcher would look for things both methodically *and* chaotically at the same time, so there had to be at least two different searchers. Based on the layered messes, it's safe to say the two searches happened at different times."

"Based on what you see here, would you say the searcher was a professional or an amateur?"

"There's evidence of both, to be honest. I'm guessing the methodical search happened first, as I only see evidence of it in a few areas, whereas the more frenzied search happened afterwards. My guess is the person who did the first search found what they were looking for."

Mary thought for a moment. "Seeing as you're in full *Sherlock Holmes* mode," Mary stood up. "Do you have any guesses as to what was taken?"

"Probably a document, his ledgers, or some papers," Malcolm pointed to the filing cabinet. "The second person spent most of their time in that area, so whatever was taken was expected to be inside there. The cabinet drawer wasn't damaged, so either it wasn't locked, or the first searcher knew how to pick locks."

"A filing cabinet… so, whatever was stolen will be eighteen cubic inches or smaller, which doesn't narrow it down much." Mary frowned. "But Zanikker's books would be a logical assumption, though we can't know for certain if the first searcher found them or not. We need a lot more information if we're ever going to start getting answers instead of more questions. I think it's time I tried to access the police accounts for our two favourite detectives to see what they know."

August 19

7:21 a.m.

"Didn't you hear what I just said?" Mary stared at a bleary-eyed Malcolm. "I found out Detective Newberg is a corrupt cop."

"Look, sorry for my lack of enthusiasm about your discovery, but it is way too early for me to be awake, and the coffee hasn't kicked in yet." Malcolm shuffled over to the kitchen and poured more coffee into his cup. "How do you know?"

"I went digging into his personal finances. I found twenty-thousand dollars in an offshore account in his name."

"So, Newberg's a goddamned crook, is he?"

Mary hummed. "Well, he's *corrupt,* at the very least, and apparently planning to escape to Thailand, by the look of things."

"Who paid him?"

"A shell company of some kind. It could take me anywhere from a few hours to several days to trace it back to a person, but I'll find it eventually."

"What about Detective Browne?"

"So far, I haven't found anything bad about him." Mary stared at her screen. "His entire financial picture seems appropriate considering his income. I don't know if that means he's clean, or if he's just unusually good at hiding his dirty deeds."

Malcolm thought for a moment. "Now I'm wondering if the cops are after Alyssa because she looks guilty, or because some wealthy puppeteer is pulling their strings and making them do it."

"Or both."

"Jesus." Malcolm took a long drink of his coffee. "And what was it you said you needed help with?"

"Are you sure you're awake enough?"

"Yeah, I'm awake enough, despite my lack of sleep because of these damned burns. As soon as your cream wears off, it hurts like hell." Malcolm sat down. "Tell me what you've been thinking about."

"Here's what I have." Mary's eyes met his. "At the risk of stating the obvious, we've been spending so much of our time dealing with distractions, that we've had no time to focus on helping Alyssa."

"We were nearly killed yesterday when our house was destroyed. That's a pretty damned huge distraction, if you ask me. We can't help our daughter if we're dead."

"I know, but it got me to thinking. It seems to me that somebody is working very hard to keep us off balance."

Malcolm thought about it a moment, then nodded. "Yeah, now that you mention it, you're right. It's as if somebody doesn't want us having any time to study Alyssa's situation, which tells me there must be something there worth studying."

"That's exactly what I'm thinking, too. So, what's the probability of the courtroom bombing and the attacks on us being directly related?"

"With our luck?" Malcolm scoffed. "A hundred and fifty percent."

"I'd say closer to seventy percent, because there's two completely different methodologies in play. The courthouse bomb was sophisticated and clever, whereas the attacks on the law firm and our house were brazen and heavy-handed. Even if the two events are tied together, they were done by at least two different people."

"Like the search of Zanikker's apartment." Malcolm took another sip of coffee. "Okay, sure, but why? Someone wanted to frame Alyssa, but not kill her. That kind of plan only makes sense if it's somehow connected to us."

"Yes, but then why go through the effort of framing her? That was an unnecessary and particularly complicated step if the goal was to just brazenly attack us, so either these are two separate events, or we're missing the connection, and that's where I'm stuck."

"Okay," Malcolm stood up and began pacing. "Now that I know where you're stuck, let's try to get you *un-stuck* by thinking it through together using an *if-then* analysis. If a bomb goes off in a courtroom, then who comes into play? I figure the cops, the feds, judges, and the city's tactical team."

"Yes, and it dominates the news cycles, both in regular media and online, so that's where everyone's attention becomes focused."

"True." Malcolm nodded. "Okay, next. If Alyssa gets framed for the bomb, then what?" He stopped pacing long enough to have another sip of coffee. "Who comes into play? Us, of course, as her parents, and we're guaranteed to be laser-focused on her well-being."

"Meaning our employer gets notified as well, so now it's on *their* radar, and maybe that is part of the objective here." Mary wagged a finger. "To get our handlers involved. This could all be about where we work and not us as individuals."

"Yeah, you may be right about that." Malcolm took another drink of his coffee. "Jesus, the bombing could also have just been a dry run for a larger attack somewhere. It's a very real possibility. The minute Alyssa's in trouble, we'd let our employer know, so they'd at least be keeping tabs on us. Maybe the thought was to distract them so something else could happen. What else am I missing? Oh, and of course, these days, if Alyssa is in trouble, we know Abby will also show up, because that's who she is. Okay, next one. If there's an attack on our house, then who comes into play?"

Mary's eyes widened. "Abby."

"Maybe, but I was thinking more about it being the immediate focus for emergency responders, which would keep them tied up and not available for another crisis elsewhere."

"No, go back for a second." Mary stood up. "You mentioned Abby."

"Yeah, what about her?"

"What if neither our employer nor the two of us are at the centre of all this after all?"

"It would be a first, actually," Malcolm scoffed. "Wait, do you think Abby might somehow be the one at the centre of everything that's happening?"

"I don't know." Mary looked at him. "Right now, I'm just thinking it through."

"Then walk me through what you're thinking, and maybe I can help to see if it goes somewhere helpful, because right now, I'm sure as hell not seeing how she could be the focus of everything that's been happening here."

Mary paced back and forth for a moment, with her index finger in the air. "Alyssa got framed for the courthouse bombing, and who was the first person to come to her aid?"

"Abby, of course."

"Anyone who knows Abby would know she'd be the first person in play, so maybe she's the target."

"No, because that wouldn't explain the attacks on us."

"Are you so sure about that?" Mary folded her arms. "Who would help Abby if she was in any serious trouble or danger?"

Malcolm nodded. "Us and Alyssa, of course."

"Right," Mary added. "Abby's support network is us, Alyssa, Marcus, and the two people at the bar Marcus owns, *The Midnight Ale*."

"Darla and Ryan?"

"Yes, Darla and Ryan, thank you. I forgot their names."

Malcolm drank the last of his coffee and set the mug down. "So, if someone wanted to go after Abby, then you're thinking they'd first need to take out her support network. Hell, that's what I'd do if I was after someone."

"Yes, exactly." Mary nodded. "And it's just crazy enough to be plausible."

"And when we're involved, crazy also means highly probable. Okay, then let's also look at the Abby angle as another possibility. And as soon as I do look at it, the first question that pops into my mind is what the connection is between Abby and Sal Zanetti?"

Mary shrugged. "I don't know."

"Have there been any attacks on Marcus or his bar?"

"I'm not sure, but I can quickly check into it."

Mary pushed her computer's mouse to its limit, with a series of rapid clicks, some quick typing, and then more clicks. "No, I can't find any news about an attack at the bar, but this could simply mean he didn't bother reporting it."

"Or, it means it hasn't happened yet and he's next on the list."

"Or it means he's behind it all." Mary walked toward the door. "In fact, he's the common link between most of what's been happening."

"Except for the ransacking of your uncle's office."

"Yes, that's true," Mary sighed. "Regardless, Marcus has been promoted to my number two suspect, just behind our friend Detective Newberg."

"If Newberg is behind this, then he could be framing Marcus as well as Alyssa."

"True, or they're working together, though I don't yet have any evidence to support that." Mary threw her hands up and let them fall. "There's way too much we still don't know, and I can't take it any more. I'm going to head out for a little while."

"Are you going to warn Marcus he could be in danger?"

"No, if he's dirty, then we don't want him knowing that we know anything, so talking to Marcus is out." Mary grabbed her keys from the top of the dresser. "We need to know if Detective Browne is clean. If he is, then maybe he can help us with Newberg. If he isn't, then I may I know how I can confirm it."

Detective Browne left the front door of the apartment complex he lived in and was surprised to see someone waiting for him. He nodded his greeting to her. "Mary Bristol."

"Detective Browne." She nodded back. "I told you I'd be in touch."

He walked toward the sidewalk and she walked beside him.

"We've left you alone, as you demanded."

"Yes, I know, and we appreciated it."

"I won't ask how you know where I live because I know you're resourceful." Browne shook his head. "I take it this is the twenty minutes you asked me for."

"It is."

"Well?" He glanced over at her. "What do you have for me?"

"I'm not a fan of taking risks like this, but what I have to talk to you about is too important." Mary reached out and put her hand on his arm. "I need you to listen to me very carefully for a moment."

They stopped walking. Mary looked deep into his eyes, studying him intensively. "If I give you the biggest, meatiest bone you could ever wish for in this case, I need you to give me your word you won't share it with your partner."

"Newberg?" Browne wore a confused look. "Why not?"

"You'll know why as soon as I explain what I have to you."

"Okay, fine." Browne shrugged. "I give you my word I'll keep him out of this, but only if it's big."

"It's big enough to be promotion-worthy, and you'd get news headlines, if you were interested in that sort of thing."

He grinned and nodded slowly. "You're going give me the name of the bomber, aren't you?"

"Yes, and you're not going to like it."

"You figured it out?"

"Most of it, yes, and it gets even better. I'm also going to give you the name of the person who I believe hired the law firm shooter."

"Great." Browne slipped on his sunglasses, as the morning sun was bright. "So, are you waiting for me to beg, or what?"

"No need for begging, but if my information pans out, I'm going to need a small favour from you."

Browne studied her face for a moment. "That's going to depend on the favour."

"I expected as much, but if I'm right, you'll be happy to oblige me." Mary was silent for a few steps. "Now, let's talk a little bit about Detective Newberg."

Alyssa had spent the night on a cot in the hospital's basement, occupying the temporarily vacated Room Three. Abby had brought her some breakfast and had then headed off to the shower. Alyssa had just finished her meal when there was a knock at the door. Alyssa froze, as she wasn't sure what to do if it was a member of the hospital staff. She was relieved when she heard a voice on the other side of the door.

"Alyssa, I'm a friend of Abigail's."

"Come in," Alyssa sighed in relief.

Alyssa looked at the woman as she entered, guessing her to be somewhere around thirty years old. "Hello," the woman said as she walked inside. "My name is Ramona."

She had shoulder-length black hair, was slender-framed, and held herself up with crutches. Alyssa wasn't able to notice anything else about the woman because of her green eyes. There were no pupils in Ramona's eyes, just two large, green irises.

"Hello, Ramona, um," Alyssa stammered. "Abby talks about you all the time. Um, it's nice to finally meet you."

"I can see you're uncomfortable with what you're looking at." Ramona smiled.

"No, I'm just… actually, yes, you're right. I'm so sorry."

"No, it's quite alright, I'm used to it." Ramona's voice resembled a whisper, albeit the loudest it could be while still being considered a whisper. "I even have a standard introduction I use for when people meet me for the first time and see my eyes." She cleared her throat. "Yes, I am able to see, but not in the light spectrum. Instead, I am able to see things in the ultraviolet and microwave spectrums, which you cannot. Yes, I can see your life energy. And yes, I've been like this for my entire life."

"I appreciate that, Ramona," Alyssa blushed. "I didn't know what questions I had, to be honest, but what you said probably answered the ones I'd have eventually come up with."

"I know." Ramona beamed. "That's the advantage of being able to read energies. I often know what people are feeling, even when they don't want me to know."

"Part of me envies that ability, but part of me thinks I'd probably be happier remaining in blissful ignorance. I'm fascinated, actually, as I'm a huge science nerd. So, you said you can see in the UV spectrum, so does that mean your vision is like a cat's?"

"In terms of just the UV spectrum by itself, then yes, it's exactly like a cat's." Ramona blinked. "If I only saw in the UV spectrum, I'd be happy, because I could go outside, but I also see in the infrared and microwave spectrums, so I can't."

Alyssa tried to make sense of this, but soon gave up. "Sorry, but I'm not getting it. Why does that mean you can't go outside?"

"I have two conditions which make an outdoor trip difficult. There are so many waves in the microwave spectrum, from radios, cell phones, and other transmitters, and it's disorienting to me. All I can see everywhere are so many pulsing waves moving in so many directions, overwhelming my eyes and rendering them useless. Years ago, I had to accept the reality that my eyes aren't suited for outside of this basement, and I'm at peace with it. The second condition is related to my skin, because I'm allergic to sunlight. I have what's called PLE, or Polymorphic Light Eruption. Artificial light sources are fine, but actual sunlight causes my skin to itch and turn red, and I get a painful rash."

"That's terrible. So... you've lived your entire life... down here in this basement?"

"More or less, though I do have unconventional ways of moving around when I want to." Mona flashed an impish smile. "The basement used to be a bomb shelter back in the Sixties, so the walls and ceiling are thick enough to prevent most transmitter waves from penetrating. That's why no cell phones or other wireless devices are allowed down here. They interfere with my ability to function."

"That makes sense. Did you hurt your legs?"

"Are you referring to my crutches?"

"Yes."

"I use them to help me walk. Hopefully in a few more years, I won't need them at all."

"Were you in an accident?"

"No, I was born into a body which couldn't function." Ramona's pupil-less eyes met Alyssa's. "I was awake and conscious, but I couldn't move my body around."

"That's horrible."

"It really was. Then, one day, around fifteen or sixteen years ago, I was able to twitch my finger. I improved a little at a time, until I got to where I am now. I'm getting better and more mobile each month. It's exciting."

"I'm happy to hear that. I can't imagine what it was like for you, being unable to move around."

Ramona grinned. "I was able to move around, just not inside of my own body."

Alyssa blinked at her, then shook her head. "I'm sorry, but once again I don't know what you mean by that."

"I could leave my body and explore in spirit form."

Alyssa couldn't help but wonder if Ramona was overdue for her medications. She took a deep breath but then didn't know what to do with it, so she let it out again.

Ramona giggled. "I can see you're distressed by what I told you."

"You just implied you could astral-travel." Alyssa nodded in an emphatic manner. "Yes, I'm a bit distressed by it."

"Because you think it's impossible, correct?"

"That's certainly the place I would start from, yes. But then you'd probably tell me it isn't impossible, it's just not yet understood, or something like that."

"Yes, that's exactly what I would tell you." Ramona smiled. "My goodness, you remind me so much of your parents. You've inherited their skepticism."

"So, Abby wasn't kidding. You really do know my parents."

"Yes, we've known one another for fifteen years."

"I'm going to have a very long chat with them when this is over." Alyssa looked at Ramona, from head to toe. "If you can really leave your body, then think of what could be learned by having scientists study you."

"We're in this basement specifically to avoid that. We don't want to end up as some kind of freak show, or being locked up in some lab getting poked and prodded against our will, or, worst of all, being weaponized and being used to harm people."

"But how is that any different from being locked up down here and being observed by doctors?"

"Because here we have anonymity, as we're not in any publicly published papers. We're also free to leave here any time we want. If we stay here, then we agree to live by the hospital's rules and consent to allowing some research to be done on us, but aside from that, we can come and go as we please. Any tests done on us are documented under pseudonyms."

"I must be missing something," Alyssa frowned. "You're saying everyone assigned to the basement has some sort of unexplained abilities?"

"Yes, that's correct."

"Then why was Abby living here?"

"The evidence we have indicates that Abigail is from another reality."

"That's not possible."

Ramona laughed. "It obviously is possible, because it happened. There was a strange electrical storm, and all sorts of bizarre things took place, and that's when Abigail appeared and met herself from this reality. So, it's not impossible, it's simply not yet understood, to use your words. For now, it's simply an unexplained phenomenon."

"Wait, back up a second," Alyssa's eyes were wide. "There are two versions of Abby?"

"There were two versions, now there's… well, it's hard to say." Ramona appeared ponderous for a moment. "There's more than one but fewer than two."

"I don't understand that at all. I understand fractions in math, but not in counting people."

"The version of Abigail in this reality is named Katherine." Ramona took in a deep breath and exhaled sharply. "It's difficult to summarize, but I'll try. Earlier this year, there was another electrical storm and Katherine disappeared. More specifically, *her body* disappeared. Katherine's spirit still lives here, so I assume she perished in the other reality. Anyway,

Katherine is able to appear in a near-solid state, so the staff from Special Projects haven't noticed she's missing. Now that Abigail is here, Katherine will stay invisible."

"The only part of that which didn't hurt my brain was where you said *it's difficult to summarize, but I'll try*. You just... you *completely* blew my mind just now. If what you said is true..."

"And it is true, every word of it."

Alyssa massaged her temples. "Then everything I learned about science was wrong."

"No," Ramona shook her head. "Not if you studied quantum physics."

"I didn't, so I'll just resign myself to never understanding this." Alyssa pointed out her door. "How many of you are there down here?"

"There are six of us, including Katherine and me, but most of them have been temporarily relocated."

"Why?"

"Because of you and Abigail." Ramona watched as Alyssa's nervous energy spiked. "There will be danger revolving around the two of you, and I don't want the other patients to get hurt when the danger comes."

"Do you mean *when* it comes, or *if* it comes?"

Ramona shrugged. "It's already on its way here, so there's no *if* involved."

"How do you know?"

Ramona smiled again. "In a way you would believe to be impossible."

"You seem strangely calm if danger is coming."

"Will my being in a panic make anything better?" Ramona shrugged again. "I just know the danger will come to this area. I can't see exactly where or exactly when, but it will be nearby and it will be soon. If it's not here today, then it will come tomorrow, but no later than that."

"Then Abby and I shouldn't be here." Alyssa stood up. "Not if it puts others at risk."

"The others are safe, I told you."

"But what about you?"

Ramona winked at her. "I'm willing accept any risks in order to help you two."

"But you just met me." Alyssa raised her eyebrows. "Why would you be willing to risk your life for me?"

"Many years ago, your parents risked their lives for me, and I'd only just met them as well. It appears their helpfulness was contagious, as I shall now do for you what they did for me."

"No," Alyssa shook her head. "I would never forgive myself if something happened to you because of me."

"That's rather silly, isn't it? Blaming yourself for someone else's decisions?"

Alyssa shrugged. "Blaming myself for silly things just so happens to be something I'm an expert at."

"Would you like to know what I see in your energy?"

"That depends," Alyssa was taken aback by the sudden change in conversation. "Is it good?"

"There is no good or bad when it comes to someone's life energy, Alyssa. It's entirely what the person does with it."

"I don't know about that." Alyssa scoffed. "I've met some pretty terrible people this year, so I can't help but think some people are just wired to be bad."

"But that's not true."

"Then I don't understand your reasoning."

"Let me explain it to you another way." Ramona's face brightened. "Think about the earth's moon, up in the night sky. Sometimes it reflects light back to the world, and sometimes it reflects darkness. People are similar – sometimes they reflect light back into the world, sometimes darkness. But the big difference between people and the moon is that the moon doesn't get to choose which one it reflects back, but people do. Everyone has a choice to either walk the path toward the light or to walk into the darkness. If you've met terrible people, then it means they made a decision at some point in their lives to walk in the darkness like that."

Alyssa reflected on this for a moment before speaking. "That just might be the most profound thing I've ever heard in my life. Okay then. As long as you promise not to mention the guys I like, what does my energy tell you about me?"

"I can see you are very much a blend of your mother and father." Ramona made a wide oval shape with her index finger. "Those tall, rounded shapes around your head mean you're a highly empathetic person with strong emotions. There's a concave shape in the middle near your shoulders, which indicates you try to suppress all the emotions you struggle with. There's some boxy-shaped layers which indicate you look for reasons, answers, and logic, and you feel distressed when you can't find them. There are some spikes emanating from your neck and chest area which indicate feelings of isolation and frustration. You worry a lot about what people think of you, and you seem to be having great difficulty with your sense of self and what your place is in the world."

"Wow," Alyssa exhaled. "For someone without conventional eyesight, you sure can see a lot."

"And I can also see how fond you and Abigail are of one another. That makes me so happy, because she really needs a good friend. So few people see the wonderful person Abigail is because they don't take the time to get to know her."

Alyssa looked away. "Abby's great, but I'll admit I didn't feel that way when I first met her. I'm kind of embarrassed by how quickly I judged and dismissed her."

"Don't feel bad." Ramona put her hand on Alyssa's shoulder. "You eventually gave her a chance. You got to know her, and then you saw the real Abigail."

"It's weird. I've only known her a few months, yet she's already my best friend."

"I'm thrilled to hear that. She hasn't had much success with friends."

"She has more friends than I have, so she's way ahead of me. She must be doing something right."

"Abby has had too much excitement in her life." Ramona frowned. "She needs to find some peace and stability."

"I can't believe I used to complain about my life being too boring." Alyssa shook her head. "After the way this year has gone, I'd give anything to go back to a dull life. Excitement is overrated and is far too dangerous." She looked up at Ramona. "I'm not going to let that excitement affect you. As soon as Abby's ready, we're going to leave here."

9:41 a.m.

"No," Sal Zanetti folded his arms and glared at his speakerphone. "I cannot allow that."

"Alyssa's future is at stake, you damned stubborn bastard." Malcolm paced inside his motel room, gripping Mary's emergency phone so tightly his fingers hurt. "I need to speak with your assistant, whether you'd prefer to allow it or not. Based on everything I've looked at, Gail likely holds at least one or two key details I'm going to need in order to solve this mystery."

"With a violent assailant on the loose, it is far too risky for me to disclose Gail's current whereabouts to anyone, whether they are police, family, or otherwise."

"But I can protect her. I have a lot of experience with that sort of thing."

"Your statement is both arrogant and presumptuous." Zanetti scowled. "Until you are able to identify the full scope and extent of the threat, it's preposterous for you to state in such absolute terms that your protection would be adequate. When you can show me *exactly* who is involved along with a comprehensive assessment of the threat they represent, I will only then consider listening to your suggestions about Gail's protection."

"Your world may revolve around certainties and guarantees, but in my world, it's all about probabilities and best guesses based on what you know," Malcolm fumed. "There are no guarantees in either of our worlds; there's only bastards and the people working against the bastards. I'm in the latter category, in case you're confused."

"Despite your frequent use of the terms, there is no *your world* and *my world,* there is only *the* world." Zanetti's eyes narrowed. "To put Gail's life and safety into a roll of the dice or a spin of a wheel would be both reckless and foolhardy. If you wish to speak in terms of probabilities, then I shall oblige you. Gail has the highest probability of safety if she remains within the arrangements I have made for her."

"Now which one of us is making assumptions?" Malcolm scoffed. "I'm a lot more capable than you give me credit for."

"It may not seem like it, but I do trust your capabilities in these more... *chaotic* scenarios. However, I prefer to trust that which I have a modicum of control over, as opposed to your more reactionary measures, which I view as a dangerous step toward societal disorder and vigilante vengeance. The moment people are allowed to put their own actions above the law is the moment society is at the greatest risk of collapse. Society makes those laws, and there's a broad consensus they are the laws which people must follow or face a specific range of consequences."

Malcolm stopped pacing and leaned against the wall. "So, you're saying whenever someone knowingly defies the laws, then they must face the punishment allocated for that specific offense, regardless?"

"Precisely."

"Then what you're saying is that the people who hid Anne Frank deserved severe punishment, correct?"

"I find your comparative and obtuse comment to be in poor taste." Zanetti massaged his temples. "Your example is completely absurd, because I am talking about democratically-elected law-makers who answer to the voters, not some abhorrent, twisted, fascist regime."

"It's not different at all, and let me tell you why." Malcolm poked at the air in front of himself with his finger. "I was born in a free and democratic society, which you might know as the United States, and we used to have laws stating black children couldn't attend white schools, and women couldn't open a bank account in their own name without a man co-signing. So I dare you to tell me more about the morality of elected lawmakers in a democratic society, but I'm going to laugh in your face as soon as you do. And don't get me started on the voters. Think for a moment about how clueless someone of average intelligence is, and then try to tell me with a straight face that they possess a firm understanding of the issues, the candidates, and what it all means in terms of how it affects the future of the country. And remember, this is the *average* voter I'm talking about. It gets so much worse when you realize if that clueless schmuck is average, then it means half of the population is even more ignorant than he is."

"You possess a most cynical outlook, albeit it is an outlook which contains points I would find rather vexing to fully refute."

"It's not cynicism; it's reality." Malcolm sighed. "In society, you have the smart people on one layer, and you have the stupid people on another layer. In between those two layers are the poor bastards who have to put up with the… wait a minute. *Layers.* In between the two layers. That's it. That's what I was missing."

"What sort of nonsense are you going on about?"

"Just let me think for a moment."

"I would imagine it may take more than a moment for that miracle to occur," Zanetti mumbled.

"I have to go and test a theory, but I need you to do me a favour. Call someone at your firm who can get me into your office's mailroom."

"I shall make the call, but why would you need to access our mailroom?"

Malcolm wagged his finger. "I may have just figured out how they concealed the bomb."

10:02 a.m.

Abby knocked on Ramona's door. "Where's Alyssa?"

"She's still in room three," Ramona pointed. "She was very stressed, so I suggested she do some deep breathing. That young woman certainly has a lot on her mind."

"She really does." Abby frowned. "I really worry about her."

"I know you do, Abigail," Ramona broke into a broad smile. "Because you're in love with her, I can see it."

"Shut up."

"And I can see she is a very special person to you."

Abby leaned against the door frame. "Yeah, she is."

"That's wonderful, Abigail. I was always hoping you'd find someone who treated you well."

Abby shook her head. "No, Alyssa's just a friend. She doesn't think of me that way."

"Whether she's a friend, a crush, or a partner, it doesn't matter. You've had other crushes on the men and women who took care of you over the years, and they've always been the people who treated you well. Alyssa cares about you and she wants to help you, so she's someone you need to keep in your life, no matter what your relationship status is."

"I am trying to keep her around, but I don't know how to keep *anyone* in my life. I know she'll run away from me eventually, because I always lose everyone who matters to me. And now I've lost Marcus, Darla, and Ryan. So, no matter what I do, I can't keep a friend."

"You've managed to keep me."

"That's true, but you're the only one." Abby stared at the floor. "Maybe I should come back here and live with you. At least then I'd have someone I could count on."

"No, Abigail, that wouldn't be healthy for you. It would also leave Katherine to be in a permanent spirit state, as there'd be questions if there were two of you down here. Do you want that for her?"

"No, I'd hate to do that to Kat, but it's way too hard for me out there." Abby walked into the room and sat on Ramona's bed. "All I ever wanted was to be independent and able to make my own life choices, but I'm not getting anywhere."

"That's not true." Ramona sat beside her and held her hand. "You've done so much, and made so much progress. Coming back here would be a step backward, and you need to keep growing and moving forward."

Abby stared at the floor. "I can't move forward because I keep failing."

"You call it failing, but I call it learning, and that's growth. And growth means you are moving forward."

"I need someone to make me functional every single morning." Abby looked at her. "You remember that, right?"

"Yes, Abigail. I do."

"I didn't really think this through, and that's one of the reasons I came here. It's too hard for me to get through every single day alone." Abby rubbed her face with her hands. "It's exhausting."

"But you won't be alone. Alyssa is very fond of you. I can see it in her energy. She'll stick with you."

"But I don't want to burden her with my needs." Abby's eyes moistened. "I can't do that to her. What if one day she looks at me and says *nope, she's not worth all the hassle,* and then leaves me as a vegetable?"

"More times than not, you have to allow yourself to be vulnerable in order to truly feel loved." Ramona put her arm around Abby and squeezed. "Especially when it's someone you have feelings for. And besides, you *are* worth the hassle."

Abby wiped away a tear. "But how do I tell her I like her without scaring her away?"

"What are some of the things you like about her?"

"She's nice to me. She helps me, and cares about me. And she smells nice."

"That's enough to start with." Ramona smiled. "Have you let her know those things?"

"Sure. I've stolen things for her. I've taken her away from danger. I've kept her safe when there was a threat of some kind."

"But you haven't *said it* to her. In *words*."

"No, I get too nervous and then I blank." Abby sighed, then wiped the fresh dampness from her eyes. "Talking is how I communicate actions, information, and objectives. When I want to communicate how I'm *feeling,* then I do things for people, and that's how they know they matter to me."

"I understand, Abigail, and that's fine. You should do it however you're comfortable. All I'm saying is Alyssa may not understand your way, so she might need to hear it. If you like the way she smells, then you could just say *you smell great,* or *you smell like a spring day,* or something like that."

"But most spring days smell like dampness and mildew."

"Don't think about it *literally;* think about it as if you were a poet."

Abby made a face. "But what rhymes with mildew?"

A young woman shuffled into the reception area to meet Malcolm. He figured she was in her early twenties, but she wore clothing he associated with grandmothers in rocking chairs.

"Hello, sir," she didn't make eye contact. "I'm sorry to bother you. Are you Alyssa's dad?"

"Yeah."

"Hi, I'm Ashley." She rocked back and forth. "My supervisor asked me to bring you to the mailroom and help you with whatever questions you have. I mean, if that's okay with you."

"Yeah, I'd appreciate that, Ashley."

"Okay, then please follow me. Only if you want to, of course. Or not at all. It's up to you, really."

Malcolm waved his hands. "Just take me to the mailroom, okay?"

They walked in silence for a few seconds, until Ashley spoke. "Is Alyssa okay?"

"I wish I knew, Ashley. I haven't heard from her, and I'm worried about her."

"I sure do miss her around here. She was always nice to me, and not everyone is, not that I blame them. So, how can I help you? I mean, assuming you even want help from me. I can find someone else if you'd prefer."

Malcolm sighed. "You own a cat, don't you?"

"Yes, three." Ashley finally looked at him. "How did you know?"

"It was more than a lucky guess. Listen, Ashley. I truly do want your help, without you second-guessing yourself. Can you do that?"

Ashley opened the door and stepped inside the mailroom, holding the door open for him. "Okay, if that's what you want."

Malcolm pinched the bridge of his nose, shook his head, and then continued. "Those unmade folding boxes over there." He pointed to where they were leaning against the wall. "I want you to show me how you fold one of those things into a box. Would you do that for me?"

"Yes, I can show you." Ashley walked over to the stack and retrieved an unmade box. It was just a single, flat, die-cut piece of brown corrugated cardboard. She held it up. "First, you fold over these two small flaps, and then you fold down the front flap, like this, and it makes the lid. Then, you take these two big sections and fold them up like this so they stick up, fold up the middle piece, then fold the two side flaps over and down, like this. Then you fold over this last big flap here, wrap it around, and then tuck it into place. This bottom flap folds over, you bend it here along the crease, and then it forms the box's base. And just like that, you have an instant box. Did I do that too fast, or was that okay? It was probably too fast, wasn't it?"

"No, it was perfect," Malcolm pointed at the box. "So there's two layers of cardboard here on the bottom, and also here and here on the two sides of the box, am I right?"

"Yes, you're right. These boxes hold up to fifty pounds, so the bottom has to be a double layer of cardboard for support, and the sides have these handles, so they need to be a double-layer as well or the box wouldn't be strong enough."

Malcolm nodded. "So, if someone felt like it, they could put something in between those two layers, right?"

"It would have to be something pretty flat, but I guess they could." Ashley stared at the box and then over at Malcolm. "I'm sorry, but I don't understand. Why would anyone want to do that?"

"So nobody would know it was there." Malcolm tapped his chin with this finger, then smiled. "You have been a huge help, Ashley. Thank you. I've finally figured out the *how*. Now I need to figure out the *who.*"

10:55 a.m.

The scent of Alyssa's skin cream sent Abby's heart fluttering, and she decided she needed to finally say something. She would try to say how she felt using words, just as Ramona had suggested. Abby's mind raced with ideas.

You smell great. You smell like pretty flowers. You smell like a spring day.

"Hey," Abby said. "You smell…" And then her mind went blank, and she couldn't remember which way she had decided to end that sentence. She ended up just standing there, and suddenly feeling as though someone had set fire to her ears.

"I smell?" Alyssa looked at Abby in horror. "This is so embarrassing. I'm sorry, Abby. I promise I'll take a shower before we leave here."

"No, great."

"What?"

"I mean the smell is great." Abby's face reddened, and her eyes began to water as she shifted her weight from one foot to another, and then back again. She tried to organize her thoughts, but she had to fight through the crippling embarrassment she was currently experiencing. She was conflicted between wanting to force the words out and wanting to run away to prevent any further feelings of humiliation. "No, I didn't mean..." Her lower lip began to quiver. "I don't…"

"Abby, what's wrong?" Alyssa stepped over to Abby and took hold of her hands. "Whatever it is, it's okay. What are you trying to tell me?"

"This." Abby wrapped her arms around Alyssa and held her tight. She then kissed Alyssa's cheek. She then let her arms drop and took a step back. *"That* is what I was trying to say."

Alyssa blushed. "Thanks, Abby. I really needed that on a day like this. You're a total sweetheart."

"And you smell like a spring day, except without all the mildew and dampness."

Alyssa chuckled. "Every time I think I understand you, I'm proven wrong. When are we leaving here?"

"We'll head out just before three this afternoon." Abby tried to stop the trembling which had begun the second she had kissed Alyssa's cheek. "There's a bus to Tacoma we can catch at a station just across the ravine."

"Okay. That makes sense." Alyssa tried to make eye contact with Abby but was unable to do so. "Um, we should probably..."

"What?"

"I mean, a few seconds ago, you..." Alyssa pointed at her right cheek. "Am I...? Was that a friendly kiss just then, or are you...? Do you....? Um... do you like me? As in, have feelings for me?"

Abby stared at the floor. "What answer will prevent you from running away from me and not wanting to be my friend?"

"We're friends no matter which way you answer." Alyssa fidgeted. "I just want to know how you feel, that's all."

"Yeah." Abby covered her face with her hands. "I have feelings for you, but I don't want to talk about it."

"Why not?"

"Because I don't know how." Abby wiped her eyes with her sleeve. "Just be ready to head out as soon as I tell you."

When he got outside the office tower, Malcolm phoned Mary. As soon as she answered, he spoke excitedly. "Good news. I now know how they got the plastic explosives inside the box. I finally have all of the puzzle pieces to explain the *how*."

"That's great," Mary smiled. "Unless, of course, it turns out you have a jumble of pieces from a number of different puzzles."

"You couldn't let me have just one moment, could you?"

"I have some good news as well," the corners of Mary's mouth turned up and she looked at her laptop screen. "I'm pretty sure I know the *who*."

"That's great," Malcolm punched the air in triumph. "Who's the *who?*"

"Detective Newberg is our culprit." Mary tapped at her screen. "I've got him dead to rights."

"With my *how* and your *who,* we're almost ready to wrap this up."

Mary nodded. "Which means the only thing we're missing is the *why*."

"I've got a source down on Hastings Street," Malcolm said as he walked. "I'm on my way to see if he's heard anything that might help me. I'll call you back after I've spoken to him."

Ryan screwed the gas cap back on his vehicle after filling up. As he stepped toward the driver's side door, he heard someone calling out.

"Ryan Kaminski."

Ryan turned toward the voice and his heart sank. "Krissa Novak. I was hoping to be wrong about your involvement."

The tall woman approached him. "I'm flattered you even remembered me."

"How could I forget?" Ryan made a sour face. "I saw one of the dismembered bodies you brought in to Marcus, so your name will be seared into my memory for the rest of my life. Are you looking for Abby, too?"

Krissa nodded. "She is the key to my mission, so yes, I am looking for her."

"Which means you're going to kill her if you find her," Ryan glared at her. "In keeping with the Novak family tradition, of course."

"No, I won't kill her, or at least I won't kill her right away," Krissa grinned. "In my experience, dead people don't give up information when tortured, they tend to just lie there unresponsive, which defeats the whole purpose of torturing them in the first place. No, I plan on taking your crazy little friend alive."

"I don't need your help brining her in. I'll find Abby without you."

"Silly boy, I'm not here to help you." There was no mirth in her short laugh. "You and I were given different missions. Marcus sent *you* to find Abby, and he sent *me* to retrieve what she stole and didn't give to him. That's the extent of our mission overlap. It just happens that I need to find her in order to find the stolen property, so I want *you* to help *me*."

"That's not gonna happen. Marcus has rules. The first one to find her brings her in, if able." Ryan looked at her with suspicion. "Do you play by his rules?"

"I will follow Marcus' rules to the letter." She leaned against his car. "It's bad for business to do it any other way. It's his money and his contract, so I'll achieve whatever objective he hires me to pursue. The methodology I employ to get that job done is up to me, as long as I get the results he demands."

"And I know you'll choose gruesome violence as your methodology, as usual."

"I like you, Ryan." She winked at him. "You say what's on your mind, and I find that so refreshing in a person. I know you're like a big brother to that crazy little Abby Lunay-tic, so let me appeal to your sentimentality. Help me take back what the little freak stole, and then this can end with a minimal amount of blood loss and broken limbs."

"I'll find Abby myself, and I'll make sure she returns Marcus' property. Then this will all get sorted out, and nobody has to get hurt or cut to pieces."

"Don't say I didn't offer."

"It wasn't much of an offer." Ryan scoffed. "I don't trust that you won't go all *slice-and-dice* the minute Abby shows up even if I did accept your offer."

"Then help me find her, so such actions aren't necessary." She grinned again. "Come on. Give me some clues, such as where you're currently heading."

"You know what I'm really good at? Keeping secrets from psychopaths."

"Okay," she nodded. "To be honest, I'm relieved you didn't agree, so I can do this the way I want. Let the hunt begin."

"Forgive me if I don't wish you luck."

"It doesn't matter to me, Ryan, because I never need luck." Her grin made Ryan shudder. "Your looney little friend Abby, however… there isn't enough luck in the world that can save her now. Which reminds me…" Krissa narrowed her eyes and smiled. "While you're here, I should ask. Are there any particular body parts of hers you specifically want to keep as a memento? I'm a whiz with a bone saw, so it's really no trouble."

"I know you're probably just trying to get under my skin, but I'll respond to you anyway." Ryan scowled. "If you harm Abby in any way, then I'll break my own rule and kill you."

"Nice try, tough guy, but you're not a killer, so your threat is as meaningless and hollow as you are." She regarded him with her cold eyes. "You've been out of the military for too long, and you've gotten soft. But let me be clear about this. If you ever threaten me again, you'll need to be more concerned about your own body parts being used as mementos."

Ryan scoffed, then opened his door and clambered into the driver's seat as Krissa made her way to her own vehicle, parked several metres behind him.

Great, he thought as he started the car. *Being followed by a homicidal sadist is another complication I don't need.*

Ryan peeled out of the gas station and began his new mission: losing Krissa.

11:52 a.m.

Malcolm had just wrapped up his meeting with his source. It was a quick meeting, as his source lived in an alleyway just off of Hastings Street, between the Regent Hotel and the Carnegie Community Centre. His source not only lived on the streets, but he was also its ears. People came to the neighbourhood – a place most locals avoid – to fence stolen goods, to buy or sell drugs, or, quite often, just to gather, as there was no other place else for them to go.

It was an area where the lack of affordable housing came second only to the lack of hope. The mentally ill, the homeless, and the addicts shared these few blocks, and everyone had their own terrible and tragic stories. The people there heard things and people talked, as there was little else to do beyond day-to-day survival, and most of the talk reached Darryl, the alleyway denizen.

Malcolm made a point of paying Darryl well, so Darryl was always happy to assist Malcolm when he had questions. Unfortunately, this time, Darryl had no helpful information for Malcolm, though Malcolm gave him some money anyway.

Malcolm made his way back up to Hastings and crossed the street. He felt as though he was being watched, but had not yet ascertained where that feeling was coming from.

He walked a block north, putting him at the city's most north-central point, which was – strangely – referred to as East Vancouver.

Malcolm never understood the local neighbourhood vernacular. In his native New York, it was organized logically, with the East Village, the West Village, Uptown, and Downtown, but here it was nonsensical. For example, the term *East Vancouver* refers to the eastern half of the city, whereas *East Van* is a specific neighbourhood. If you're looking for the western section of Vancouver, it's the *west side,* unless you're downtown, in which case it's called the *west end.* If you ask how to get to West Vancouver, you will end up in a completely separate city across the harbour, and for reasons nobody seems to know for certain, the city of West Vancouver was established *north* of Vancouver.

Hastings Street, the busy street Malcolm had just been on, runs along the northern edge of Vancouver, which is not, according to residents, located in *northern Vancouver.* There are no northern or southern sections of Vancouver; there's only the west side, east side, and downtown.

Hastings starts in *East Van* and runs through downtown. The infamous and notorious Main and Hastings intersection — also located in the geographically northern section of Vancouver — is never referred to as being in *northern Vancouver*, and is instead referred to as being part of the *downtown eastside*.

It was Malcolm's theory that Vancouver's traffic was unusually bad because nobody can ever truly be sure what direction they're going.

Malcolm had that *being watched* feeling again, so he stopped and turned around. About twenty paces behind him, he saw Detective Browne following him.

"Malcolm Mercer," Browne said as he approached. "I need a minute."

"Ugh." Malcolm rolled his eyes. "Sorry, pal, but I've already surpassed my monthly quota of conversations with sanctimonious detectives, so maybe call in a month or two and I'll try to fit you in."

Browne held up a brown shopping bag. "Even if I brought a peace offering?"

"That depends. What is it?"

"I thought you'd appreciate me playing into the stereotype." Browne opened the bag and held up a decorative box. "I'm a cop, and I went to the doughnut store and bought a half-dozen."

"I like the humour and the gesture, so you've got my attention." Malcolm took a few steps toward him. "I can't eat the doughnuts, but we can talk."

"You don't like doughnuts?"

"I like the kind of snacks that would cause my cardiologist to tilt his head down, look over his glasses at me, and then sigh while shaking his head."

"And yet you appear to be in remarkable health for your age, despite those snacking preferences."

"You're not getting what I'm saying." Malcolm looked at him. "I love doughnuts and other tasty crap like that, but my wife has told me they're no longer my snacks of choice, no matter how much I may think otherwise. So, my snacking preferences are different from the snacks I actually get to eat. At some unknown point in my life, my wife obtained a veto over most of my diet, and she doesn't let me eat junk food."

Browne chuckled. "It's a good sign, Mercer. It means she wants to keep you around for a long time."

"Then it just goes to prove she must be crazy." Malcolm grinned. "You married?"

"Yeah, six years now." Browne nodded. "So, I can relate to what you said. I really did buy the doughnuts as a peace offering, but if I'm being completely honest, it was also so I had a work-related excuse to enjoy something that I want to eat."

"Yeah, Mary wants me to be a vegetarian. She says I'll live longer, but it would really only make me more willing to die."

"Wives are funny that way. They try to keep us alive and healthy, and we make jokes about it and pretend we hate it, but we'd be lost without them." Browne shook his head. "Men are weird creatures sometimes, aren't we?"

"Come with me."

The two men walked together in silence. Malcolm opened a door which led into an indoor plaza, which was ringed with small shops and take-out places. Malcolm led Browne up a flight of steps and into a narrow, secluded hallway where there was a bench. Malcolm sat and motioned for the detective to join him.

"Alright, Detective Browne." Malcolm sat back and folded his arms. "I've lowered my guard and you've put me at ease, so check off those two boxes on your interrogation procedure checklist. We've established a rapport, so check off that box, too. So, skip ahead to the part where you tell me what this is all about. What are you *really* wanting from me?"

Browne chuckled. "I can't blame you for being suspicious, but I've recently discovered you're not the bad guy in all this. The doughnuts aren't part of some interrogation tactic, they're an olive branch."

"Huh." Malcolm studied Browne's face and then slowly nodded. "I've never heard of doughnuts made from olive branches before. What will they think of next?"

"While you're busy being a smartass," Browne put the box on his lap and opened it, "I'm having one."

Malcolm's mouth began to water while his pancreas began to prepare for the worst. "Well, I'm sure your wife would be furious if she knew I just sat here and let you eat all of those unhealthy treats yourself. The least I can do is have one, to keep you from getting into too much trouble."

Browne grinned. "I'd really appreciate that."

Malcolm selected a chocolate doughnut with sprinkles and took a large bite. After a few moments of blissful chewing, he looked at the doughnut and then at Browne. "It's too bad sugar and fat are so damned unhealthy."

"Couldn't agree more." Browne smirked. "It's unfair that the things that shorten your lifespan are also the things that make life worth living."

"If there was a god who truly loved us, then Brussel sprouts would be unhealthy and sugar would be good for you." Malcolm took another bite.

"It's all relative." Browne pulled out a small paper napkin and wiped his mouth. "Genetics, lifestyle, family history, and all that. It all plays a role."

"Yeah. I had a buddy once, years ago." Malcolm swallowed. "He was from England. He lived to be ninety-eight on the four British food groups of sugar, salt, fat, and overcooked vegetables. That lucky bastard."

"That's exactly what I'm saying," Browne nodded. "You never know, right?"

"Okay, so before my blood sugar spikes too high, I have to ask this. You said you discovered I'm not the bad guy, but how did you figure that out?"

"There's quite a story there."

"Maybe there is, but I have attention-span issues, so can you summarize it for me in two sentences?"

"In that case, I'll do better than that." Browne glanced at him. "I'll tell you in two words."

"That's even better. What are the two words?"

"Five Eyes."

"Not sure that does the trick." Malcolm took another doughnut when Browne held out the box to him. "I mean, even if I wore glasses that would only get me to four eyes. In order to hit the five mark, I'd somehow have to add a monocle into the mix as well."

"No, smartass, and you know *exactly* what I mean." Browne returned the box to his lap and selected another doughnut for himself. "The intelligence services of Canada, the United States, Britain, Australia, and New Zealand are part of the *Five Eyes Intelligence Oversight and Review Council,* or *FIORC.*"

"Yeah, I've heard of them."

"I should hope so." Browne nudged Malcolm with his elbow. "You and your wife are part of it. You're both coordinators, and you work with each of the five countries."

"Was that your desperate shot in the dark, or something?"

"Listen, I needed to know more about you and Bristol, so I could determine whether you two and your daughter were innocent victims or guilty parties in all this mess. Let's be realistic here. If people like you and your wife were parties to the bombings, then we'd need to call in some heavy-duty help to deal with you."

Malcolm nodded as he chewed. "Your thinking makes sense, but how does one thing connect to the other?"

"You're not the only one with well-connected friends, you know," Browne glanced at Malcolm. "I have a buddy who knows a senior federal court judge, and he set up a phone call between me and that judge. At first, the judge wouldn't tell me a damned thing, until I told him what was happening and what was at stake. He then sent me a non-disclosure agreement to sign, and said he'd only help me once I signed it and submitted it to him for review. The NDA I signed states I'll get a minimum two years in prison if I breathe a word of this to anyone except you, and I don't have the right skin tone to make an orange prison suit look good on me. The judge told me to back off and give you room to operate, which is why I came to you with a peace offering. He also told me that you and your wife are part of Five Eyes, and that you've made some enemies along the way. You don't have to answer this, but I'm too curious not to ask it anyway. Are you still out in the field?"

Malcolm thought for a moment, then decided this was one of those *what the hell* moments. "Hardly ever. I've gotten too old to be in the middle of the action, so these days I tend to get the less-demanding tasks. My knees and back aren't what they used to be, I had hip-replacement surgery five or six years ago, and I take pills for my blood pressure, so I'm hardly front-line material anymore. Despite that, trouble seems to catch up with me anyway, and I end up front and centre of every damned disaster that happens." Malcolm locked eyes with Detective Browne. "So, it looks like you now have the whole story."

"Yes, and I think you'll like how the story ends. I'm convinced your daughter was framed."

"Yeah?" Malcolm raised an eyebrow. "So, then what are you going to do about it?"

"That's up to you. You can trust me or not, but the more you tell me, the more I can help you."

"Alright. Walk with me, and I'll tell you what I can."

"Sounds good."

The two men stood up.

"But," Malcolm grinned, "if we're going to be walking and talking, then we're each going to need another one of these to keep up our strength."

Both men took a doughnut, then Browne put the empty box into the nearby trash bin.

"Your wife thinks my partner is a dirty cop." Browne shook his head. "She showed me what evidence she has on him. It took me by surprise at the time, but now that I've had time to really think about it, I'm convinced she's wrong."

"Newberg's your partner." Malcolm shrugged. "I can understand you defending him."

"No, it's not just that," Browne nibbled at his third doughnut. "Sometimes Newberg rubs people, including me, the wrong way. He conducts investigations in a manner I often find wrong-headed, but he gets good results, and I've never known him to take a bribe or knowingly arrest an innocent person.

He's a bit of an old-school cop, and can be a bit of an ass sometimes, but he's not corrupt."

Malcolm shrugged as he ate. "Being an old-school ass hat doesn't make him innocent."

"Actually, in this case it does."

"Oh, I can't wait to hear this explanation." Malcolm took a bite of his doughnut and listened, as Browne shared what was on his mind.

12:02 p.m.

"Krissa Novak?" Ryan all but shouted the name into his smartphone's wireless device, as he spoke to Marcus Coltrane while driving. "You sent a member of the Novak family after Abby? You know what they're like, Marcus, they're maniacs. They're the types who would use a tactical nuclear strike to kill a mosquito. When was the last time one of the Novaks brought someone in alive? Or, for that matter, in fewer than four pieces? And Krissa's the worst of them."

"I've only used the Novaks seven times in the past fifteen years, but I've gotten favourable results on each and every one of those occasions." Marcus whistled. "It's really hard for me to argue with a hundred percent success rate. Listen Ryan, I pay people to get results for me, even if it means having to wait for dental records. As long as I get enough pieces to confirm they're no longer part of the equation, then I'm satisfied. Krissa is the one who is most likely to get this job done quickly and effectively, so in my view, she's the *best* of the Novak family."

"She's a sadistic, violent, sociopath, and Abby doesn't need such a heavy-handed approach. This is pure unnecessary overkill."

"She's not after Abby, she's going to retrieve what Abby has in her possession."

"You're not understanding what I'm telling you," Ryan snapped. "If Krissa finds Abby, then things will go badly. Give me some time, and I can convince Abby to hand it over without the Novaks being involved."

"You know me, Ryan, I'm a nice guy. In most cases, I prefer a softer, more polite approach, but in this case, the kid gloves had to come off."

"But Abby's one of us, and she's been loyal to you for years, so she doesn't deserve this."

"It may seem that way to you, but it's only because you never take a moment to step back and look at the big picture."

Ryan checked his rear-view mirror, and didn't see Krissa's car. "Then why don't you go ahead tell me what you think I'm not seeing."

"Play it out logically in your head, and keep in mind the priority is to be *proactive* and not *reactive,* okay?"

"Yeah, fine."

Marcus cleared his throat. "Okay, so, I sent Abby out to steal something for me, and she ended up keeping it for herself. The item is something of great importance to me, so that means I need to get hold of

Abby so I can get it back from her. Are you with me so far?"

"Yeah, so far, so good."

"So, if I go after Abby to retrieve my property, who can I count on to meddle and interfere with that effort?"

Ryan nodded. "Alyssa and her parents."

"One hundred percent correct. Therefore, her parents need to be busy with bigger problems."

"Such as Krissa Novak."

"I knew you'd catch on if I laid it out for you." Marcus grinned. "This is why we make such a good team."

"We are a good team, boss, and that team includes Abby. I want this incident to get worked out so we can all go back to how things were. I'm going to find Abby, get your property back, and then we're going to move on, without the need for violence or any harm being done."

"There is a large part of me that hopes you succeed, Ryan, and I truly mean that. You're a good man, but if you want any chance of this having a happy ending, then you'd better find Abby now."

"I will." Ryan scowled. "And I'm going to bring her in alive."

"Then you'd better hope you get to Abby before Krissa does."

Ryan disconnected the call and stomped on the accelerator.

2:03 p.m.

"Thanks, Ramona," Alyssa hugged her. "I can't begin to tell you how happy I was to finally meet you."

Ramona regarded Alyssa when the embrace ended. "Leaving here will not prevent the danger from happening."

"I know," Alyssa nodded. "But it changes *where* the danger happens."

"You're safer here." Ramona paused, hoping the words would resonate. "Abby is also safer here."

"Safer, maybe, but not *safe*." Alyssa frowned. "If we stay here, then we put you and others at risk. If we leave, then it's only the two of us in danger."

"Don't worry," Abby hugged Ramona next. "I'll find another place to hide, but Alyssa and I have to leave. I'll go to the storage room upstairs and get some supplies together. I want to be out of here by three at the latest."

"But where will you go?"

"The Seattle-Tacoma area." Abby released Ramona. "There's more places to hide in a big urban area amongst a few million people. You're sure you can keep the book safe here?"

"Yes, absolutely," Ramona held Abby's hands. "Katherine wants to say goodbye to you as well."

"I know." Abby nodded. "She's in my head right now, actually."

"Yes," Ramona smiled. "I can see her there with you."

"She says my brain and body are showing signs of healing. That's the best health news I've heard in years." Abby pulled away.

"That is happy news," Ramona gave Abby's hands a gently squeeze.

"Is Kat the one helping me heal?" Abby zipped up her small backpack.

"No, but she says she might be able to help you. Maybe that means you should stay here longer."

Abby smiled at her. "No, but that was a nice thought. Alyssa and I will grab a quick sandwich from upstairs, and then head out while we still can."

"Good luck," Ramona said as the two climbed the basement stairs. She watched as they left through the door into the hallway of the hospital's main floor. When the security door shut, Ramona wiped away a tear. "I hope they don't die."

2:38 p.m.

"So that's where you've been hiding," Malcolm muttered under his breath as he read the email he'd just received. He clicked *reply* and typed *I owe you. And thanks again for the doughnuts* then hit send. "I should have known."

Malcolm closed his recently-purchased laptop computer and sat back in the small, plastic chair in his motel room. He took a sip of his coffee, which by then was lukewarm, while he processed the information he had just learned.

"That slick bastard," Malcolm chuckled and shook his head. "I didn't know he had it in him."

Mary stepped into the room. "Who are you talking about?"

"Oh, nobody; I was just thinking out loud," Malcolm put his mug back on the table. "I'm always impressed by how silent you are. I didn't even hear you unlock the door and come in. How the hell do you do that?"

"A lot of the jobs I've been sent on over the past twenty-five years necessitated my sneaking into places I wasn't supposed to be in, as you know, so I'm glad I'm still in good form. So, what are you hiding from me?"

Malcolm wore a blank expression. "What do you mean?"

"You only say things like that out loud when you don't think I'm around, and then when you see me, you try to get me to focus on my own lack of sound instead of what you were muttering about."

"Listen, I had a very interesting chat with Detective Browne today."

"And I'm very interested in hearing all about that," Mary walked toward Malcolm and then stopped in front of him. "But that will come *after* you tell me about what was going on before you knew I was here."

"How can you be so sure what I was muttering *wasn't* about Detective Browne?"

"Because you wouldn't have asked me that exact question just now if it was about him. And if you're this eager to change the subject, then it means there is clearly something even more important going on than Detective Browne. So, who's the slick individual with the parents out of wedlock?"

"I promise to tell you once I get something confirmed."

"You said you didn't know someone had it in them." Mary folded her arms. "What was that about?"

Malcolm shrugged. "Sometimes, you think you know a person and then get surprised, that's all. People are like that."

"Somehow I feel there's a lot more to this conversation than your observations of human behaviour. Confirmed or not, is there something you're hiding that I should know about?"

"Come on," Malcolm wore a sour expression. "There is no way for me to answer that without lying to you, so don't ask me that."

"That was Malcolm-speak for *yes, Mary, I'm hiding something from you*. So what are you not telling me?"

"I can't tell you what I'm not telling you, or I'd be telling you, which defeats the purpose of not telling you in the first place, so I'm not telling you."

Mary thought for a moment. "Just so I'm clear, are you not telling me *for now*, or not telling me *ever?*"

Malcolm shrugged. "It depends entirely on what I can confirm in the next hour. I got a tip from a reliable source, and I just need to verify the information they sent me. So, right now, at this moment, my plan is to not tell you at all, but I know how these things work. Instead, I'm trying to not tell you for as long as possible."

"Is it something about me?"

"No, I promise it isn't about you."

"Then is it about you? Or my family?"

Malcolm glanced at the ceiling as he looked for the right words. "It could be about your family, but, again, I need to confirm that, first. Look, this isn't a game of twenty questions."

"Of course it isn't."

"Oh, good."

"I won't need twenty questions to find out what's going on."

Malcolm frowned. "I suddenly hate everything about this conversation."

"Is it about Antonio?"

"You know what? Until a few minutes ago, I would have bet a lot of money it was *entirely* about him, but it isn't. Not directly, anyway."

Mary shifted her weight from one foot to another. "So, he isn't suing me for attacking him?"

"No, he's… wait, what?"

"Never mind. Is it about Sal?"

"He is… certainly a person of immense significance in this, so yes." Malcolm blinked at her. "Did you seriously attack Antonio?"

"It's still my turn to ask the questions."

"When do I get a turn?"

"I'll give you a turn once I'm finished with mine."

"And how long is your turn?"

Mary locked eyes with him. "Until I say otherwise."

"Did I mention how much I'm hating this conversation?"

"Yes. And now that I've answered four of your questions, it's back to being my turn again."

"Wait, what?"

"I know you and Uncle Sal don't get along, but you made some minor progress last month. Haven't you two buried the hatchet yet?"

"No, because he'd probably try to bury it in my back." Malcolm scoffed. "I wouldn't trust him with a rubber spatula, let alone a hatchet."

Mary pulled out a chair and sat down across the small table from Malcolm. "Whether you like it or not, he's family, so we all need to try and get along."

He looked at her. "So, you're saying you want me to be nicer to him from now on, is that right?"

"Yes."

"Then fine." Malcolm stood up. "Consider it done."

He walked toward the door to leave when Mary called out to him. "Hold up."

I was so close, Malcolm thought as he had his hand on the door latch.

"It just occurred to me that we didn't finish our conversation."

Damn.

She stood up. "Like I said, I know you and Uncle Sal don't get along, but I am suspecting there's more to what you're hiding than just the current state of your relationship." Mary walked over to him. "You need to tell me what it is."

He turned to face her and leaned his back against the door. "Look, Mary, I know you hate it when I say things like this, but your uncle's side of the family are all career-driven, ambitious go-getters, who lust for power positions, and don't let anything stand in their way."

"What's wrong with that?"

"Nothing, except the part about not letting anything stand in their way."

"The Zanetti family has always overcome obstacles and adversity." Mary moved closer to him. "They're resilient and determined people. Let's face it;

there are always people out there who will try to pull you down."

"I know, but it's the *way* they sometimes deal with obstacles I take exception to. Their methods aren't always civil."

Mary raised an eyebrow at him. "That sounds incredibly strange coming from you, of all people. What methods specifically are you objecting to?"

"Mary, listen to me." Malcolm put his hands on her shoulders and looked deep into her eyes. "If I tell you what I'm pretty sure is happening, then at best you'll be terribly upset, and at worst, it could have a catastrophic effect on your relationship with the entire family. You were just recently brought back into the family after more than thirty years, and this could seriously jeopardize that. Please, I'm asking you – *pleading with you* – to trust me and let the subject drop."

Mary nodded. "I trust you completely, so I will let it drop."

"Thank you."

She held up a finger. *"For now."*

"Only for now? Please tell me *for now* is measured in weeks or months."

"No, it's measured in one second intervals. If there's so much as one, single second where I sense something is off, or where I think there's danger to someone, then *for now* expires, and then I need you to tell me what's going on, and I mean full and immediate disclosure. Do I have your solemn word?"

"Yeah, sure, you have my word."

"Good," she narrowed her eyes. "Because I definitely sense something is off, and I believe there's imminent danger because of it, so now you have to tell me everything."

Malcolm squeezed his eyes shut. "I can't believe I didn't see that one coming a mile away, and I walked right into it."

"So, spill it."

He looked at her and sighed. "Like I said, I still have to confirm my suspicions, though I'm ninety-nine percent certain they're true."

"Don't make me wait," she gently slapped at his shoulders. "Just tell me what you think is happening."

"You were right," he said with a sharp exhale. "The thing I was trying to keep from you is about Sal Zanetti."

"What did you find out?"

"Your uncle is going to prison."

3:07 p.m.

As soon as Alyssa had finished her sandwich, Abby grabbed her by the wrist, and pulled her through the hospital basement toward a door at the far end. "We have what we'll need now, so let's move quickly."

"What am I missing about this sudden sense of urgency?"

"You heard what Ramona said earlier," Abby pushed the door open and they stepped into a long, narrow, dimly-let tunnel. "If she says there's danger coming, then I want to be as far away from here as we can possibly get."

"Where does this tunnel go?"

"To the small park across the street. We'll cut through it, cross the street, then head down into the ravine."

They arrived at some concrete stairs and both began the ascension.

"Why are we going to a ravine?" Alyssa was breathing hard.

"Because on the other side of that ravine is the bus station." Abby opened the door at the top of the stairs. "We'll get two tickets to Tacoma, and it's a direct trip with no stops. We need to put some miles between us and here."

"You're scaring me."

"Good." Abby led Alyssa across the tiny room and out through the secure door which opened into the park. "There's a lot to be scared of right now. Come on."

They ran across the small park, then made their way across the narrow street, and then disappeared into the thick cluster of trees which edged the road. The two made their way down the heavily-forested ravine to a small creek, which meandered around the stones and thick grass. Despite the warmth of the day, it was quite cool near the creek.

As they stepped across the creek, they heard a rustling sound. Both Abby and Alyssa looked to their left and saw, emerging from the bushes, a burly, bearded man whom they both recognized.

Ryan stepped forward and nodded at them.

Abby deflated. "I can't believe you found me so quickly."

"Then you somehow forgot I'm good at finding people, especially when it comes to you." Ryan pointed toward the hospital. "This is the last place you'd want to be, so it made sense it would be the first place you'd go to in order to hide from me."

"I should have figured that," Abby winced. "I haven't been having a lot of success, Ryan. I know you said to keep away from you, but now that you're here, I really need your help."

"With what?"

"I didn't realize until recently how much I depended on you to get me organized." Abby shrugged. "I didn't bring what I needed in order to be on the run like this."

"Listen," Ryan held up his hand. "Before we do anything else, I need you to answer a question for me."

"What?"

"Are you going to finish the break-in job Marcus sent you to do?"

Abby looked confused. "But I did finish it."

"No, not quite." Ryan stepped forward. "You only did half of the job. You stole the item, but you haven't given it to Marcus yet."

"That's true, but he lied to me, so he's not getting it."

"What lie did he tell you?"

Abby wrung her hands. "He said if I stole the book for him, the bar would stay open, and then you and we would still have our jobs."

"Then it wasn't a lie, because everything you just repeated to me is completely true."

"No, not completely." Abby kicked a small stone. "Marcus made it sound like I was saving the bar and our jobs, but getting the book is only to keep *Marcus* out of prison. It has nothing to do with the bar, and nothing to do with us."

"Abby, listen to me, and think about it." Ryan locked eyes with her. "If the cops get their hands that ledger, they'll raid every one of Marcus' businesses, including the bar, and shut them all down. If Marcus gets thrown in prison, you and I get thrown out of work, plain and simple. What he said to you was true."

"Okay, maybe, but he also told me there was no point in explaining any of it to me because it was beyond my comprehension." Abby's words were laced with contempt. "He treats me like an idiot, and I hate that."

"Okay, you're right, he was being an ass to you." Ryan made a conciliatory gesture with his hands. "You are bright, and I agree he should have explained it to you, for sure. But that aside, the net result is the same."

"He always assumes I'm stupid, and I hate it when he thinks he can manipulate me into doing whatever he wants."

"Abby, please." Ryan clasped his hands together. "Just give him the ledger and complete the job so we can all go back to how things were."

"No, and now it's your turn to listen to me, okay?" Abby took a step toward him. "Would you agree that Marcus and the bar are safe as long as the police don't get their hands on that book?"

"Well, sure, but--"

"Then I finished the mission." Abby glared at Ryan. "Like you said, the net result is the same."

"But where's the ledger?"

"It's hidden, so Marcus doesn't have to worry. I put it where nobody will find it."

"Abby, listen to me." Ryan took in a deep breath. "He needs the ledger in order to conduct business."

"Then he can go through me to get access to it when he needs it."

Ryan shook his head. "When Marcus didn't hear from you, he sent someone else to do the job."

Abby shrugged. "Then he's wasting his money, because they won't be able to find what I already have."

"No, you're completely missing my point." Ryan looked wretched. "Marcus sent Krissa Novak to find you in order to get his ledger back. Do you remember who Krissa is?"

"I think so. Is she the one I used to refer to as *Doctor Dismember?*"

"Yes, that's definitely her."

"Then I already know about that." Abby waved her hand in a dismissive way. "I followed her into the law firm the other day. She's the main reason I got Alyssa out of there."

"If Krissa finds you, she going to torture you and then kill you in order to get hold of that ledger."

Abby frowned. "Well, that kind of ruins my day."

"Wait, what?" Alyssa's eyes were wide with alarm. "This is the first I'm hearing about any of this. Why didn't you tell me?"

"I kind of did." Abby looked at her. "I did tell you that there was a lot to be scared of. *Doctor Dismember* is the sort of nightmare your other nightmares have at night." Abby then turned back to face Ryan. "We're on a tight schedule, so we have to go now. Thanks for the warning, buddy."

"I'm not here to warn you, Abby." Ryan took a few steps closer. "I'm here to make sure you get the book, and then we're all going to see Marcus together so we can straighten this mess out before anyone dies."

"But you've got to know I'm not going to do any of that, right?" Abby glared. "I'm not giving him the book."

"You're not going to have any choice in that, because I'm not able to take no for an answer." Ryan put his hands on his hips. "What you're doing right now? This whole thing with Alyssa? *It's over.* Please, Abby. I'm worried about you as your friend. Hell, we're as close as family, so let me protect you."

"Protect me?"

"Yes," Ryan nodded. "I know it doesn't seem like protection, but it really is. If I bring you in, then you live. If Krissa brings you in, it will be in pieces. *Very dead pieces.* I just saw Krissa a few hours ago, and she confirmed she's after you."

"Wow," Abby scowled. "You should have led with that. I'd have gone into hiding sooner."

"I won't let her harm you. You're the little sister I didn't have."

"But you have a younger sister named Maureen."

"That's different. She's the little sister I *did* have."

"I still don't understand any of this, or see why it's such a big deal." Abby stamped her foot. "Just tell Marcus the book is safe and that's that."

"That's not good enough for him. You know how nuts he gets when there's a loose end. He's become obsessed with getting the ledger back in his own hands, and he's willing to go as far as he has to in order to achieve that. Krissa searched Zanikker's place, and she didn't find the ledger, so he went into full panic mode."

"Zanikker did have the book, but I took it from his filing cabinet so it would be safe. That's why she didn't find it."

"I wish you'd told me you retrieved it. Marcus was worried the Zanetti lawyer had it."

Alyssa raised her hand. "But why would my uncle have it?"

Ryan glanced at Alyssa. "Because he's your relative, and Marcus has been on edge about the influence you've had on Abby lately."

Abby scoffed. "He's just being a cranky-pants, which for him is normal."

"Yes, but he's gone into full-blown paranoia mode now." Ryan rolled his eyes. "Cranky, yeah, we're all used to that, but he's gone all gangster over this. He was worried you were going to betray him, so he sent Krissa to Zanetti's office to look for the ledger. When it wasn't there, Marcus figured you still had it."

Abby nodded. "And he's right. I do have it."

"But he also thinks you're planning on keeping it."

"Then he's right about that, too."

Ryan rubbed his face with his hands. "But why would you choose to keep it, especially now that you know about all the danger it's put you in? This isn't only about the way he made you feel, is it?"

"Okay, fine." Abby moaned. "To be honest with you, there is a little more to it than that. I want the book for leverage. As long as he's worried about the book, he won't double-cross me, and he won't hurt Alyssa or her family."

"If that's the case, then you need to know your leverage isn't as good as you think it is." Ryan made a face. "Krissa already burned their house down and made an attempt on their lives."

"Hang on, what?" Alyssa's eyes grew wide and she stared at Ryan. "Are my parents okay?"

"As far as I know, yes," Ryan rubbed his face. "Sorry, miss, you weren't supposed to hear that from me."

"My home burned down?"

"Yeah, Krissa Novak reduced it to ashes. I'm sorry to be the one to tell you." Ryan shrugged and turned back to face Abby. "Listen, Krissa is going to hunt Alyssa and her family relentlessly until you return the book to Marcus. That's his leverage, so it's greater than what you have. As long as the ledger is out there, you're in danger, Alyssa's in danger, and her parents are in danger. Krissa will make more and more attempts on their lives until everyone's dead or until Marcus gets his ledger back."

"So, you think I should give the book back?"

Ryan guffawed. "Hell yes, it's a no-brainer. It's the only way to end this without someone getting killed."

"If someone has to get killed today," Abby fumed, "then let's make sure it's Krissa, and not any of us."

"None of us are killers, Abby, except for Krissa, and she's damned good at it. If we try to take her on, it won't end well, and one or more of us will die." Ryan pointed at Alyssa. "Are you willing to risk her life too? No, you're not, so giving Marcus his ledger back is our only safe move."

"No, you're wrong," Abby sneered. "There's another way to end it. I can tell the cops where to find the book, and I can let them take Marcus down."

"Abby please. If Marcus goes down, then he'll make sure the cops take me down, too."

"But you don't do the type of stuff Marcus does."

"No, but I've done plenty of other things." Ryan swallowed hard. "Marcus has enough dirt on me to keep me very motivated to ensure you don't make a move against him. He has dirt on you, too, you know."

"I don't care what happens to me," Abby fumed. "I'm twenty-five years old, and *literally* nobody thinks I'll live to see thirty. Most people are surprised I'm still alive at twenty-five. I'm living on borrowed time, Ryan, so if I need to give up whatever small amount of time I have left in order to help Alyssa, then that's exactly what I'm going to do. At least then my life will have mattered to somebody."

"Your life matters to me, Abby." Ryan's voice was softer. "It always has."

"Then you shouldn't have come here," Abby snapped. "You'll end up leading her right to us."

"No, I lost her, don't worry."

"I doubt it." Abby grabbed Alyssa's wrist. "You're an awesome bouncer, Ryan, but you're nowhere near experienced enough to lose someone like *Doctor Dismember*. It's not your skillset, but it is hers. Now, Alyssa and I are leaving right now, and if you value our lives, you'll let us leave, because you've signed our death warrant."

"How magnificently insightful." Krissa stepped into view from behind the wide trunk of a nearby tree.

Ryan turned and glared at her. "How the hell did you find me?"

"I put a tracker on your car at the gas station while I was distracting you."

Abby frowned at Ryan. "I told you."

"Well, you're too late, Krissa. I found Abby first, so you know Marcus' rule." Ryan held up his index finger. "The first one to find her brings her in."

Krissa stepped closer. "Oh, I'm familiar with the rules, Ryan, and I know his rules even better than you do. I know you found your looney friend first, and you have my respect for that."

"Okay, so then back off so I can take these young ladies into my custody."

"No, I'll be taking them into *my* custody."

Ryan shook his head. "No, no, we both agreed to abide by Marcus' rules."

"And I am." Krissa's grin was menacing. "His rule states the first one to find Abby brings her in *if able.* You may have been the first to find her, but in a few seconds, I'll be the first one to find her who will still be *able.*"

In one, swift movement, Krissa pulled out, aimed, and fired a Taser at Ryan, hitting him squarely in the chest. His body went into a series of rapid spasms before falling to his knees. In the time it took for Ryan to fall to the ground unconscious, Abby leapt into action, tackling Krissa.

Krissa dropped the Taser, and rolled herself out of the way of Abby's attempt to grab onto her. Both Krissa and Abby were quick to get back on their feet, and the two squared off. Alyssa finally snapped out of being stunned with surprise, and stood beside Abby.

"Get behind her," Abby growled.

Alyssa tried to circle behind Krissa, but Krissa kept stepping back, so as to keep both women within her line of sight. Alyssa tried again, and Krissa adjusted, but as she did so, Abby attacked. Krissa saw her coming, however, and delivered an elbow into the side of Abby's face. Abby managed to land a blow to Krissa's ribs, causing Krissa to stagger, and as she did so, Alyssa leapt at Krissa, who hadn't yet regained her balance. Alyssa was able to get a firm grip on Krissa and sent her tumbling across the small creek-side stones.

With two quick blows, Krissa was able to break Alyssa's hold and then roll back onto her feet just in time to see Abby's bloodied face up close as Abby thrust her knee into Krissa's stomach. Abby attempted to deliver her elbow to the back of Krissa's neck, but Krissa twisted around, grabbed Abby's elbow with one hand, and deflected the blow, knocking her off balance and Abby fell awkwardly into the creek.

Alyssa came in for the next attack, but Krissa feigned a dodge, and as Alyssa came in to deliver a snap-kick, Krissa grabbed hold of Alyssa's lower leg and spun her around. As Alyssa's momentum sent her into a tumble, Krissa delivered a sharp kick to Alyssa's side.

Krissa then turned and attacked Abby, who had only just managed to get back on her feet. Krissa faked a kick, and as Abby fumbled to block it, both of Krissa's fists connected with Abby's torso, and Abby landed hard on the wet creek bank.

Krissa then turned and smiled at Alyssa, who was dizzy and barely able to stand.

"I need looney Abby alive, but you, on the other hand, are just in my way." Krissa approached Alyssa.

"I need to know something," Alyssa blinked hard. "Why did you burn my house down?"

Krissa shrugged as she drew nearer. "I needed your parents distracted."

"By burning down the house?"

"I'm not one for subtlety, and it worked, because they were thoroughly distracted after that." Krissa stopped walking. "Listen, girlie, I'll make you a one-time offer, and it expires in ten seconds."

Alyssa shook her head, still trying to get the cobwebs to clear. "What's the offer?"

"Don't resist me, and I will make it quick and painless for you," Krissa drew closer, a knife appearing in her hand from a hidden sheath. "On the other hand, if you decide to cause me any further trouble, then you're five minutes away from begging me to kill you."

"Those aren't tempting options." Alyssa stammered.

"Maybe not, but they're the only options I'm offering you."

Alyssa sighed, deflated. She then nodded. "I'm not big on long, drawn-out pain, so I'll do my best."

"Wise choice." Krissa raised the blade waist-high. "Now hush, and it will all be over in a few seconds."

Krissa stepped forward, and as she neared Alyssa, she thrust the knife toward her. As she did so, Alyssa's leg sprung up in a snap kick and the toe of her shoe connected sharply with Krissa's wrist, and the knife cartwheeled away, landing in the creek. Krissa grasped her newly-injured wrist with her other hand and glared at Alyssa. "I see you've chosen slow and painful."

"I wasn't happy with your choices, so I added kicking your ass to the list of choices, and selected it instead."

"Stupid child." In a flash, Krissa lunged at Alyssa, catching her off guard. Krissa's fist flew at Alyssa's face, and Alyssa barely recoiled enough to avoid the blow, but the sudden backwards motion caused her to fall onto her back, knocking some of the wind out of her. She gasped for breath as Krissa came in for another attack.

Abby attempted to stand up, but staggered and fell back down. She could only watch with a sense of helplessness as Krissa delivered a series of sharp blows to Alyssa, crumpling her to the ground. Krissa then grabbed Alyssa by the arms and dragged her over the stones toward the creek. She then pushed Alyssa's face into the water. Alyssa, now weak and clinging to consciousness, was unable to resist, and she felt the cold sting of water as she was immersed.

Abby screamed and managed to get onto her unsteady feet. Operating solely on a mixture of rage and adrenaline, Abby charged at Krissa and tackled her. After a brief struggle, Krissa was able to toss Abby aside and stagger to her feet.

"I'm no longer finding this fun, so it's time to end this."

Krissa reached to her holster, but her hand found nothing to grasp. She looked down at the empty holster, then at Abby, who sat on the rocks with Krissa's own gun aimed at her.

Abby's eyes narrowed. "I'm not having fun either." She pulled the trigger and the shot hit Krissa in the upper chest. She spun around and fell upon the creek bank, groaning in pain and clutching her fresh injury.

Abby scrambled over to Alyssa and pulled her head out of the water, then rolled her over onto her back. Abby began resuscitating Alyssa, working on her feverishly until she eventually spat up water and began to cough. Abby then held Alyssa close and burst into tears. "I thought I lost you."

She rolled Alyssa onto her side, to ensure she didn't choke on anything. She was too busy tending to Alyssa to notice what was happening behind her.

Krissa Novak kept one hand pressed against her bullet wound, while her other hand reached down into her thigh-high stockings and retrieved a knife from a hidden sheath. She had a clear shot at Abby's back, so she brought the knife up into a throwing position. Before she could throw it, the back of her head was struck with great force by a length of tree branch, and she slumped over, motionless.

Ryan tossed the branch aside and knelt down beside Krissa. "You're not so tough without a weapon, are you?"

He slowly stumbled over to where Abby and Alyssa were. Abby flashed him a weak smile.

"Thanks, buddy. As soon as I can stand, I'll go and grab that book from its hiding place."

6:44 p.m.

Marcus Coltrane could hear the commotion from his office. He looked at the security monitor on his desk and saw the police swarming in through the front and rear doors, with their guns drawn. He leapt up from his chair and went over to the false wall and activated a hidden release mechanism.

He stooped down and passed through, then closed and latched the door behind him. It was a mere three steps to the hidden door which led to his adjacent property, which he had set up as a fortune-telling business. He unlatched the door and stepped through into the tiny kitchen in the unit. He was startled to see his kitchen was occupied.

"It's so lovely to see you again, Marcus," Mary smiled with feigned sweetness.

"Hey, Marcus." Malcolm had his 9mm Beretta aimed at him. "Raise those hands a little higher for me, if you don't mind. I'd like you to meet a couple of friends of mine. This is Detective Newberg, and at the far end is Detective Browne."

"What is this?" Marcus stared at Newberg.

"It's an arrest," Newberg smirked. "Imagine my surprise when these two fine people," he pointed at Malcolm and Mary, "forwarded me some photos of your ledger which they were sent by one of your former employees. You have quite a bit of explaining to do."

Newberg approached Marcus and put him in handcuffs and sat him down in one of the chairs in the kitchen. Browne placed a recording device in front of him and made him aware of his rights. He finished with a single question. "Care to make a statement?"

"I was set up," Marcus gestured with his chin in Newberg's direction. "By him."

"Yes, and I have to admit, you had me fooled at first," Mary gave a nod. "I totally bought it. You knew I'd do my research on the investigating detectives. It took some digging, but I discovered a transfer of twenty-thousand dollars in Newberg's name being placed into an overseas account. The transfer was relayed through multiple hubs, making it challenging for me to trace. Once I uncovered it, it was all there. The multiple transfers, the encryption, and the digital alias all pointed to Detective Newberg."

"I want to speak with my lawyer." Marcus shook his head. "This is completely absurd. If there's a dirty cop in this room, then he should be the one in handcuffs, not me."

"And if there was a dirty cop, he would be in cuffs." Browne said. "As soon as Ms. Bristol told me what she'd found, I knew it all had to be planted."

"Planted specifically for *me* to find," Mary nodded. "And I was in such a hurry, and was so eager to find what I was looking for, I didn't question it when I found it, and that was a huge mistake on my part. I didn't realize it was placed there so that Detective Newberg would take the fall for the bombing, the mercenary, the attack on our home, Alyssa's arrest, and everything else."

Malcolm put his gun away and glanced at Marcus. "You found out which detective was assigned as the lead on the case, but you didn't actually look at him as an individual. I mean, look at Newberg. He's sixty-two years old, uses pens and notepaper when taking statements, and still uses a ten-year-old flip phone."

"He's a real luddite." Browne scoffed. "Newberg can barely use email when we're in the office.

In fact, he doesn't even use a bank machine because he hates the digital world."

Newberg scowled at Browne. "Do you *really* need to be piling on as well, here?"

Mary continued. "So, all that electronic subterfuge didn't add up. When I accessed his personal accounts, I should have noticed right away that he uses cash for everything."

"And," Browne grinned, "you made it look as though Newberg had plans to flee to Thailand, when he can't handle heat and humidity. And the guy has never traveled outside of the province. He's a total xenophobe."

"Do you mind?" Newberg scowled. "You're making me look bad here."

"Well, admit it. You do need a vacation."

Malcolm looked at Browne. "You got everything from here?"

Yeah." Browne nodded. "Newberg and I are going to take Mr. Coltrane back to the station with us. We're going to ask him an astonishing number of difficult questions in our most uncomfortable interrogation room. I hope his lawyer gets a nasty headache from it all."

"Okay then," Mary looked at Newberg. "Now, if you'll excuse us, we have a family reunion to attend."

7: 11 p.m.

Mary pulled the car into the long driveway. She parked on an angle in front of the Mercedes to block it. They saw Sal Zanetti by the vehicle, frowning at them.

Mary and Malcolm exited their car and approached Zanetti. Malcolm pointed at him. "You and I need to talk, pal."

"Then make it quick, as I am in haste."

"You've been a naughty boy, so let me spell it all out for you, and why the police will need to make a prison cell available for you."

"There is no need for your tiresome theatrics." Zanetti put a small bag and his briefcase into the Mercedes. "I am fully cognisant of what I have done. I have already written my resignation from the firm and have been busy making arrangements to ensure whatever needs to be taken care of is fully arranged."

"I see you have a bag packed." Mary gestured toward the briefcase. "Are you planning on going somewhere?"

"Yes, actually." Zanetti glared at her. "At the time of your arrival, I was mere moments from departing for the police station, to turn myself in."

"You needed to pack a bag for that?"

"If you must know, the bag contains the books I had borrowed from a colleague, and I was going to return them to their owner before I surrendered myself to the authorities. The briefcase contains relevant documents as well as my signed confession."

Malcolm scoffed. "What exactly do you need to confess to, aside from witness tampering and obstruction of justice?"

"Those are merely two of the crimes I willfully committed."

"Jesus." Malcolm shook his head. "Keep things in perspective, will you? There's been murders, assaults, terrorism, blackmail, theft, fraud, and a dozen other felonies committed, and you're worried about the little things you did?"

Zanetti looked at him with contempt. "They are hardly what one could refer to as *petty*. It is not as if I had been cited for jaywalking, or not putting coins into a parking meter. I am a lawyer, and as such, I must be an example to others that laws must be followed. If there are no consequences, then what is the point of laws existing in the first place?"

"For the rich and powerful to avoid, mainly." Malcolm folded his arms. "You know, I agree the stuff you did is serious, but it's minor compared to what I thought you were involved with."

Zanetti cast a glance toward Mary. "What is he prattling on about?"

Mary shrugged. "We were thinking you might have financed a plot and had a police detective on your payroll, but I very recently discovered it wasn't you."

"I should never do such nonsense." Zanetti paused and then looked from Mary to Malcolm. "If you are aware I had no part in whatever plot you were talking about, then why are you here?"

"I'll tell you." Malcolm stepped forward. "Before you leave, I want you to tell me where Gail is."

"I shall do nothing of the sort."

"She helped to frame Alyssa, so you need to know I'm the sort of person who would hunt down someone like that."

Zanetti shook his head. "Gail *unknowingly* helped to frame Alyssa. She was duped into aiding that sociopathic woman miscreant. You'd be foolishly targeting an innocent, just to fulfil your ill-advised vendetta against a sweet and harmless person."

"According to you, wouldn't I be targeting an *alleged* innocent? I noticed how you're all in favour of the fancy legal terms when it suits you, but as soon as you're the one on the hot seat, you're less concerned about the burden of proof. No matter what you *allege,* Gail should be my next target."

"You will not experience any success, as I have sent her into hiding."

"Yeah," Malcolm sneered, "I already know about that, as it happens, but I was hoping you'd have had a shred of decency and confess to us what you did. You were a naughty boy for sending her on an indefinite sabbatical to Liguria, Italy, under an assumed name."

"I shall neither confirm nor deny that."

"You don't need to confirm it, because I already confirmed it on my own." Malcolm locked eyes with him. "Listen, you probably don't know this about me, but years ago, I made a pretty successful career out of tracking down fugitives, so finding Gail was easy for me, once I knew what to look for." Malcolm glanced briefly at Detective Browne. "And the police verified it for me. You know why I did fugitive recovery for so many years? It's because I took such joy in bringing them in, so they could get what was coming to them. I'm as good at that as you are at estates law, maybe better, so what makes you think I won't go to Liguria and bring Gail back?"

"Two reasons come to mind." Zanetti straightened his tie. "The first is that she was a blackmail victim, so based upon what I know about you and the way you view the world, you would not wish to bring her back to a place where she would face unjust consequences, simply because she was trying to protect others. Gail was coerced and manipulated, and she was led to believe nobody would be hurt as long as she cooperated. Gail would never have complied had she known Alyssa would be put into harm's way. Alyssa is family, and Gail knows I would find it unforgivable if anyone compromised the safety and well-being of a family member."

"Fair enough." Malcolm's nod was subtle. "And the second reason?"

"She's in the protective care of the Zanetti and Bellantoni families, so no matter what proficiencies you may have had in your previous vocation, you would be unlikely to get past the family."

"So, Gail is staying with your relatives?" Malcolm nodded. "Wow, so she's getting a punishment *worse* than prison. Nice twist."

"I shall overlook your glib comment."

"As it happens, I agree with you, and Gail should be left alone and not prosecuted." Malcolm watched Zanetti's face closely. "You've made the case as to why, but that doesn't mean I plan on forgiving her for her endangerment of Alyssa, whether it was intentional or not."

"Only the petty would hold onto a grudge like that."

"Then the petty people of the world consist of me, ninety-nine percent of all parents in the world, and you."

Zanetti cleared his throat. "Just to be clear, I never asked Gail to do… those unfortunate and misguided actions she *allegedly* took part in. I would have preferred none of it to have taken place at all. A violent and dangerous woman accosted my assistant and showed her photos. These were pictures of Gail's two adult children and her six grandchildren. That wretched woman said she would make sure the children vanished, one by one, unless Gail did *exactly* what she was told to do. If Gail notified the authorities, they would all die horrifically. I truly wish my assistant had come to me, as I could perhaps have aided her before it came to what it did, but she was much too frightened to risk it."

"Let me guess. " Malcolm scoffed. "That same woman then gave Gail a box, and told her to make sure it was delivered to the courthouse. When Gail saw a box already on the counter, she simply did a quick two-second swap when Alyssa's back was turned."

Zanetti stared at Malcolm for a moment before answering. "And how did you deduce that?"

"It was the only answer that fit the clues and circumstances." Malcolm folded his arms. "Your assistant probably thought *'that's it? I put a label on the box and swap it out and everyone is safe? Great. Who could possibly get hurt by a box?'* Well, as it happens, it did more than hurt your colleague, it killed him as well as his client, and it was only by pure luck it didn't kill more people. There was a wide, thin layer of plastic explosives in the bottom and sides of the box, sandwiched between the two layers of cardboard. Alyssa worked beside it, stacked documents on top of it, and then wheeled it to the courthouse. At any given point in that period of time, she could have been killed by that box. After the bomb went off, Alyssa had to once again fear for her life and experience new hells and trauma. Speaking of that, I have no clue how scarred this whole thing will leave Alyssa. So, take a moment and think about everything that happened since Gail's lapse of judgement. Our house was destroyed, many lives were put at risk, some lives were lost, Alyssa was in danger, and it was all put in motion because your assistant did as instructed without questioning the potential consequences of her actions or alerting anyone."

"Gail is a tactical thinker, not a strategic one." Zanetti stared at his car door for a moment. "She looked at the threat in front of her and dealt with it. She makes an exceptional assistant because she deals with the day-to-day minutia, and leaves the planning and strategic thinking to me. It's hardly Gail's fault some wicked woman came along and forced her to do something terrible, far beyond what she was able to handle, so adjustments needed to be made for her benefit."

"Adjustments?" Malcolm emitted a sardonic chuckle. "Like, hiding a witness? Compromising a criminal investigation? Do you actually hear the words coming out of your mouth right now? Flexible morality, citing technicalities, and circumventing laws for your own objectives? You know, all of a sudden, your world is sounding an awful lot like my world."

"As I have already told you, there is no *your world* or *my world,* just *the* world. I may find the world's darker sections, where you choose to inhabit, to be abhorrent, but even a broken clock is correct twice per day. The corners of the world I prefer are far from perfect, as you took great pains to point out to me earlier. However, as you also asserted, sometimes, the people breaking the laws are the ones fighting against a perceived injustice."

Malcolm nodded. "So, you wouldn't kick Rosa Parks off of the bus after all. Huh. There just might be hope for you."

"That fire in your soul serves you well, and I respect the passion with which you look after Mary as well as your devotion to her." Zanetti glanced briefly at Mary, then back at Malcolm. "Regardless of how and what I think of you as a person, you're a good husband to her. Misguided, ill-behaved, and oafish, perhaps, but a good husband nevertheless. Perhaps there's some Zanetti in you after all."

"There's no need to get nasty."

"You joke, but like it or not, you are a part of this family." Zanetti wagged his index finger. "The things I have done to protect both Gail and Alyssa may seem abhorrent to you, but had you needed it, I would have done the same to protect you as well. If not for your sake, then for Mary's."

Malcolm shook his head. "That sounds to me a lot like a code of honour, so it's not abhorrent to me at all. I'd take whatever steps were necessary in order to protect the people I cared about as well. I respect the ideals behind what you did, but remember what you said about Gail? You wished she had come to you earlier, right? Well, I wish you'd come to Mary and me earlier, too, and let us know what the hell was going on. We may have been able to find a better way to get it done. A way, I might add, where you wouldn't end up needing to trade in your expensive wardrobe for a single orange jumpsuit."

Zanetti sighed. "It's no longer relevant, as what is done, is done, thus making any hypothetical discussions moot. I obstructed justice, so where there is crime, there must also be punishment, or else we would lose our civil society."

"I'd argue there's nothing civil about it, but that's beside the point now. What about the topic we discussed recently?" Malcolm stepped closer, with Mary by his side. "You just said sometimes people who break the laws are the ones fighting for justice."

"And I stand by my assertion, but it is not applicable in my case." Zanetti's voice became softer. "My actions were not borne out of a desire to help an oppressed demographic, or to address some outrageous social injustice. I acted out of the selfish desire to help someone close to me who was in a distressing predicament, and I knowingly aided and abetted in the disappearance of a key and vital witness in a police investigation, which supports a charge of obstruction, to which I shall plead guilty. I had a choice in what I did, whereas Gail and Alyssa did not. They were unjustly entrapped, whereas I was not. I willfully exceeded the limits of the law, so my actions must bear the appropriate consequences. Now, if there's nothing else, I must be on my way to see the police."

Malcolm patted Zanetti on the shoulder. "Wait, I do have one last question before you go."

"And what is your question?"

"Have you ever been sedated?"

10:26 p.m.

Emergency Rooms are often populated with a number of self-proclaimed handy-men and *do-it-yourselfers,* who watched a two-minute video on the internet before commencing with complex home repairs or intricate electrical work, which they were utterly unqualified to do. The money they had hoped to save often ends up being a fraction of what the medical treatments and rehabilitation expenses end up being, yet this sort of thing somehow remains a popular option.

There are often two thoughts which go through the minds of Emergency Room patients. One of those thoughts is *there must be a less embarrassing way of explaining this to people.* The other thought is *what if that had been the end?*

Ryan Kaminski was currently pondering the latter, as he lay in the hospital bed. Abby was visiting him in his room, having had snuck out of her own hospital bed and using a set of crutches to get around.

"Come on, Abby," Ryan groaned. "Marcus' bar may be shut down, but I'm hoping to open my own at some point in the future, and I could use your help."

"You'll find people to work for you when the time comes, so you won't need me." Abby tried to smile, but the pain in her face made her regret it. "Darla and the others did all the real work. I just did the illegal stuff for Marcus."

"You're my friend, so if you ever need a job, keep in mind the offer stands."

Abby winked. "Thanks, buddy, but this is good-bye."

"Wait, you can't go yet." Ryan sat up a bit, wincing from the soreness in his arms. "I need to ask you a couple of things first."

Abby leaned against the door frame. "Go ahead."

"When am I going to get the ledger from you?"

"I can safely say never." Abby shrugged, then made a face due to the pain. "I sent pictures of some of the pages to Alyssa's mom so she would have what she needed to take down Marcus. She made a deal with one of the detectives she was working with. In exchange for the evidence, I get immunity for every crime I've committed, and get a clean slate so I can start over. They didn't ask for the pages showing the stuff you did, so I didn't offer them."

Ryan frowned. "Alyssa's parents are making it so damned difficult to hate them."

"I know." Abby nodded. "They start to grow on you, and before you know it, you're having meals with them."

"Do you think I'll get some sort of immunity arrangement as well?"

"I don't know, Ryan. Alyssa's mom arrived in town about an hour ago. All I know is she's going to talk to you about some stuff."

Ryan nodded. "I guess I'll have to wait and see what she comes to me with. Now that I'm no longer working for Marcus, I'm looking back at everything I did while at the bar, and it makes me wonder what the hell I was thinking all those years."

"Yeah, there's nothing quite like a near-death experience to snap someone out of a stupor." Abby held up a finger. "Unless, of course, it goes badly, in which case it becomes a *death experience*, which means being in a stupor would be an improvement. You can't really snap out of being dead."

"I suppose that's true," Ryan grinned. "So, what about you? If you're saying no to the job and goodbye to me, then I'm guessing you have a career in mind."

"Yeah. Maybe I can use what skills I have to help people. I might open a detective agency or something."

"You're kidding, right?"

"Not really," Abby thought for a moment. "I'll have to work out the details, but it's one of the options I've been considering."

"If you do, then I hope it works out for you."

"Me too." Abby grinned, despite the discomfort. "Good luck, buddy."

Abby managed an awkward about-face, then hobbled out of the room and down the hall. Mary was leaning against the wall, waiting for her.

"Go easy on him." Abby pleaded. "I know he deserves whatever charges you decide to press, but… he was my friend. And he saved me and Alyssa from ending up dead in a ravine."

"I know, Abby." Mary's hand brushed a strand of hair out of Abby's freshly-damp eyes. "He's not necessarily an evil person just because he's done some evil things."

Abby nodded. "I'm going back to Alyssa's room."

"Wait, in all this commotion I haven't had a chance to thank you yet." Mary leaned in and kissed Abby on the forehead. "Alyssa told me everything. She's alive because of you. Her father and I will forever be in your debt. You're family to us."

Abby smiled and then used the crutches to make her way down the hall.

Mary took in a deep breath and let it out slowly. She then walked into Ryan's room.

Ryan nodded at her. "Yeah, Abby said you'd be stopping by."

"Yes," Mary gritted her teeth. "If things had turned out differently, we wouldn't be talking at all right now. I am going to attempt to do this as calmly and rationally as I can."

"I guess that's as good as I can expect." Ryan sighed. "The floor's yours, so say your piece."

"Your former boss, Marcus Coltrane, is a lot of things, but a computer genius isn't one of them. In order to frame that detective, he needed to delegate that task to someone, and I finally traced it back to you."

"Yeah." Ryan looked down at the bedsheets. "I'm not going to lie about it at this point. Not after everything I've found out over the past few hours. It makes me sick knowing Marcus was the one who arranged for Zanikker to be killed. I swear on my life I didn't know he'd go that far."

"Zanikker was going to cut a deal and hang Marcus out to dry." Mary wore a look of disgust. "Marcus found out, and then put his elaborate bombing plan into action. The bomb blast worked better than he anticipated. Not only did he kill Zanikker, but he also got one of the lawyers helping him."

"I promise you that I didn't know about the bomb."

"I'm inclined to believe you, but I have another question for you." Mary folded her arms. "Was framing Alyssa for the bombing by design?"

"I don't know if it was at first, but once it happened, Marcus kept adding fuel to that fire."

"And you didn't try to stop him, did you?"

"No, ma'am." Ryan looked up at her. "Listen, if you want honesty from me, then you're going to have to hear some things you don't want to hear, and a large part of that is going to be about how much your daughter is disliked, both by Marcus and myself. The only reason I cared anything at all about Alyssa was because Abby did. I'd have happily left her at the bottom of that ravine, but it would have broken Abby's heart, and I couldn't live with myself if I did that. Once I got Abby to the hospital, I went back for Alyssa and got her checked in as well."

"And why are you in the hospital?"

"I'm not as young as I used to be." Ryan shrugged. "After dropping off your daughter, I collapsed in the Emergency waiting room. They're keeping me overnight for observation, but so far, they think it was just exhaustion and dehydration." He gestured toward the IV drip to his left.

"Why did Marcus want to frame Alyssa and send her to prison?"

"Because she's a bad influence on Abby, that's why. Well, I suppose technically, she's a *good* influence on Abby, but that's bad for the type of business he had. That *we* had."

"And I suppose he didn't like that Alyssa was weaning Abby off of the alcohol dependency. He had less control over her that way."

"No, that was one thing Marcus appreciated. She drank so much, it was expensive to maintain her needs. On the other hand, he was pissed off that Alyssa wouldn't share with him the chemical fix she invented for her."

"That's because it hasn't been perfected yet." Mary shrugged. "She would have shared it with him eventually. But I'm guessing Marcus hated that Abby was more dependent on Alyssa than him."

"Yeah, exactly," Ryan nodded. "As long as Abby had an interest outside of the bar, Marcus considered it an unnecessary distraction. I was happy for Abby, but it took away from her work."

"Don't get me wrong, I appreciate all of your honesty and cooperation thus far." Mary narrowed her eyes. "What I don't understand is *why*. I figured the minute I started asking you questions, you'd demand to see a lawyer."

"Abby's my dearest friend." Ryan stared at Mary. "I love her like a sister. It looks like Marcus is going to end up in prison, and it's looking more and more as though I will as well. Abby can't function on her own, so she needs to be taken care of. I figure if I cooperate, you'll make sure she wakes up fine every day."

"Fair enough. That does make sense."

Ryan looked at her. "This is the part where you tell me whether you will or you won't."

"I told Abby just a couple of minutes ago that we consider her to be family now." Mary looked deep into his eyes. "That means she always has a home with us, and if anyone touches her, we'll mess them up in a really profound and meaningful way."

"Good." Ryan nodded. "Can I ask you something?"

"Sure."

"Was the missing three million dollars accounted for in Marcus' ledger?"

"Yes, it was all there, except for the twenty thousand to incriminate the detective, and what he used to hire a mercenary. Do you know who the mercenary was?"

"Yeah, her name's Krissa Novak." Ryan rolled his eyes. "And she's a real piece of work."

"Where can I find her to have a little chat about her behaviour?"

"You can't." Ryan paused to think about his next words. "But I can promise you that she won't torch anyone's house ever again."

"What did you do to her?"

"Me?" Ryan feigned surprise. "She must have hit her head on something at one point or another and then succumbed to her injuries. Last thing I remember, she was hurting Abby and your daughter, and maybe a little karma found its way to her."

"I see," Mary nodded. "Alyssa and Abby both mentioned a ravine. Would it be safe to assume the mercenary is still down there?"

"She could be anywhere, even possibly on the creek bank, where the creek bends around the big boulder." Ryan studied Mary's face for a moment. "So, what happens now?"

"This." Mary removed a pair of handcuffs from her back pocket and clamped one end on his right wrist and the other on the metal bedframe. "I'm going to stay here with you until the local police arrive. They're going to watch you until the extradition papers are filed so you can be brought back to Canada for prosecution. And *that's* when you'll be given a choice. You can testify against Marcus and plea your way to a reduced sentence, or you can be his loyal right-hand man, stay silent, and spend the next few decades in prison."

Ryan looked at her. "I didn't hear any allegations in there about my alleged involvement regarding a mercenary having an alleged ravine accident."

"Are you testifying against Marcus?"

Ryan nodded. "Hell yeah."

"Then I'm not aware of any mercenary or accident."

The faintest of grins appeared on his face. "I'm really starting to see what Abby sees in you. And the allegations of someone setting up a cop to take the fall?"

Mary shrugged. "I'll let the police look into that themselves. Detective Newberg has notified his Lieutenant that he's retiring in two weeks, so he has his happy ending. That's good enough for me."

"So, if I testify against Marcus, I'll face a couple of felonies, and a handful of misdemeanours, and then that's that?"

"You'll do some prison time, but how much will depend on what kind of deal you can make and your behaviour while behind bars." Mary sat on the end of his bed. "Listen, this will be kind of awkward, but I need to tell you this straight out. Once you're out of prison, whenever that may be, I'll be following your career with great interest to make sure you're a model of good behaviour. You're going to obey the laws, help little old ladies to cross the street, and live an exemplary life, or… well, can you extrapolate from there, or do you need me to spell it out for you?"

"No, I think I got it." Ryan stared at the handcuffs. "You're being more than generous, which leads me to ask this. Is it because I helped to save Abby and Alyssa, or is it also because you see some potential in me?"

"If I'm being honest, it's because of Abby and Alyssa. Abby thinks highly of you, so I'll offer you this. Pay your debt to society, and then I'll help to make sure you land on your feet so you can show me your potential."

"Here's my counter-offer. You take care of Abby, and I'll take care of myself."

"You don't want my help?"

Ryan thought for a few seconds. "I might, now that I think of it, but let's see what happens."

Mary stood up. "I think we have a deal, Ryan."

August 20

Sal Zanetti opened his eyes and blinked a few times. He was lying down and staring at a ceiling he didn't recognize. It was made of smooth plaster and had been painted an off-white, though it seemed to also have a curious hint of amber in it. He frowned, annoyed as he was by the grogginess in his head.

He remembered an argument with Mary and her husband – such an impossible man – and then the two of them attacked him. He remembered Malcolm grabbing his arms while Mary stuck him with some sort of needle. He shuddered as he recalled the event.

Zanetti remembered struggling until his knees buckled, and then being gently lowered to the ground. The last thing he remembered before blacking out was a rather rude comment from Malcolm to the effect of *'Jesus, he's a lot heavier than he looks'*.

But where had they taken him?

He realized he was in a bed. No, he observed, not *in* a bed, but *on* a bed, and with a blanket of some sort covering him. But whose bed was it? It certainly wasn't his own, it was much too narrow. As he lay there, his nose alerted him to an unexpected aroma. It smelled like stewed tomatoes… and oregano. There was definitely oregano in that scent.

He propped himself up on his elbows and looked around. Based on the number of superhero pictures on the walls and the plastic figurines on the shelves beside the bed, he deduced he was in a child's bedroom.

As he pondered this, the door opened and he heard a child's voice. "He's awake."

"Giorgio?" Zanetti blinked at the young boy. "Where the devil am I?"

Giorgio turned toward the hallway and yelled. "Grandma, he's awake. Can I have my room back now?"

Zanetti smiled as he saw his wife Isabella enter the room. She hurried over to him, sat on the bed, and then threw her arms around him.

"My dear Isabella." Zanetti kissed her cheek. "Where am I, and what is happening?"

"You're at Roberto and Andrea's place." Isabella patted his cheek. "You're with the family."

"That's more than twenty miles from where I last remember being." Zanetti sat up. "How did I get here?"

"Your niece brought you here."

"Which niece? Was it Mary Bristol?"

"Yes, she drove here, dropped you off, and then said she had to rush off to some place in Washington State."

Sal's frown deepened. "You are never to speak her name to me again. I want nothing to do with her or her husband ever again. As far as the family is concerned, they are dead."

"You're being a stubborn old mule, Sal."

"They brought me here against my will."

Isabella covered her face with her palm. "And you were going to allow yourself to be arrested against *my* will."

"We discussed this at length, my dear."

"No, you told me what you wanted to do at length, I told you not to do it, and then you went ahead and did it anyway." Isabella shook her head then emitted a short sound of disgust. "I've spoken to the family, and we will not allow you to do this."

"There are laws, so I must do what is right."

"No, *this* is what's right." Isabella pointed at him, her finger an inch from his nose. "And don't you dare shun Mary and her husband for bringing you here. They spoke to me about the situation ahead of time."

"And you gave them your blessing to proceed with this abduction?"

"Yes, because it wasn't their idea, *it was mine*. I reached out to Mary on my own, because you were being pig-headed, and they both agreed to help me save you from yourself. Don't you dare try to shun them, or you'll be the one needing to be readmitted into the family."

"I cannot even begin to fathom what I am hearing from you. You allowed them to drug and kidnap me?"

"You were *transported,* not kidnapped, and be grateful." Isabella wagged her finger. "Malcolm's first choice was a tranquilizer dart big enough to drop a gorilla. Be thankful I convinced him to go with a low-dose syringe, or you'd be sleeping for another three days. At the rate you're complaining, I should have let him go with the dart. It would have been much quieter around here."

"Was there anything else which took place during my involuntary slumber which may affect my blood pressure?"

"Yes, you'll be pleased to know that Gail boarded a plane a few hours ago, and is on her way back home."

"Finally, some good news. It appears, then, that my sending a letter to the firm outlining my actions and announcing my resignation was somewhat premature."

"No, Sal," his wife patted his arm. "You didn't send a letter, you *wrote* one. You gave it to our security man to mail for you, and I took it off his hands."

"Where is the letter now?"

"I have it in my bureau drawer." She smiled at him. "You can still resign if you wish to, but think it through first. If you decide to retire, then I don't want you moping around the house, touching my herb garden, or interrupting my quiet time. I wouldn't stand for any of that."

"Indeed, indeed," Sal nodded, then looked at her. "Perhaps two or three more years at the firm would, indeed, allow me to better prepare for a more gradual transition toward retirement."

5:03 p.m.

Karl Oberman, manager and owner of the Barclay Court Motel, was grappling with a brand-new feeling, as he stood in his front office while Detective Newberg spoke to him. When Richard Newberg first arrived, Karl felt his stomach tighten and he felt a certain sense of anger and disgust.

But then Newberg dropped the news he was not only retiring, but moving away. Karl had never felt elation with Newberg in the room, but he believed it was a feeling which was worth getting used to as soon as possible.

"So, anyway, we're in the process of buying a cabin up north at Cache Creek, and..."

Karl wasn't hearing any of Newberg's retirement plans. Instead, he thought about Richard Newberg being out of his life, and moving a four-hour-drive away, and he couldn't help but smile. Newberg spent the next eight minutes boasting about his planned life of retired fishing and leisure in a small town, but Karl felt no envy. Just relief. And joy. There was definitely lots of joy.

As Newberg left, Karl beamed in delight as he went back to the spreadsheet on his computer screen. As he tried to remember where he had left off, a curious thought struck him.

He recalled the conversation he'd had a few days ago with a soot-covered man who had demanded no interruptions. Karl remembered the part of the conversation where the man had told him if he was happy with Karl's discretion, he'd owe him a favour.

And then came the news about Newberg's retirement...

"Best favour I could have asked for."

7:31 p.m.

Abby sat up in her hospital bed, which was beside Alyssa's bed in their shared room. Abby made a lot of groaning noises as she manoeuvred herself into a more comfortable position.

"I hurt in more places than I knew I had."

"Tell me about it," Alyssa moaned. "No, wait. Just so you know, I wasn't being literal, so don't *actually* tell me about it. I have enough pain of my own to deal with at the moment."

"I'm going to need some more meds."

"They gave me a pretty big dose, but it's already wearing off." Alyssa managed to turn her head enough so she could see Abby. "Speaking of medicine, I haven't given you your dose of my herbal mix since yesterday, yet you're carrying on a conversation with me. Have you been drinking?"

"A little bit, yes."

"Wait a minute." Alyssa wrinkled her forehead. "Who got you functioning this morning while I was out of it?"

Abby's face showed a weak smile. "I was able to wake myself up."

Alyssa sat up, despite the protests of her many injuries, and pivoted around so she was sitting on the side of the bed with her legs dangling. "Seriously?"

"Yup. It took me more than two hours, but I did it. I then bribed the porter to smuggle me in a bottle of vodka."

Alyssa closed her eyes. "I'm afraid to ask, but how long did the bottle last you?"

"I still have it." Abby gestured toward her backpack, which was on the floor beside her bed. "I've only had a few sips. Just enough to keep me working."

"I'm so proud of you." Alyssa smiled. "Is this Kat's doing?"

"I don't think so. Kat told me she noticed some healing inside of my brain, so I think it's your homemade stuff that's helping me. So, that's good news."

"No, that's *great* news, but I want to change the subject for a minute." Alyssa took in a deep breath. "Before you went to visit Ryan's room yesterday, you said you were thinking about opening a detective agency. Were you serious about that?"

"Maybe. I don't know yet. It might just be the lack of alcohol or the painkillers talking. At this point, I'm just pitching ideas out loud to see which ones I like." Abby looked at her. "So far, it's the idea I like the most."

"Unless I'm missing something, the other ideas you mentioned were circus clown, pharmaceutical test subject, and town drunk. You didn't exactly set the bar high with those career ideas. Keep looking. But if you do decide to become a detective, then I'll support you, one hundred percent."

Abby's face lit up. "We could work together in the agency."

"Sorry to disappoint you, but no." Alyssa's face grew more serious. "Listen, Abby... I need to thank you for everything you did for me these past few days. I appreciate every single thing you do for me, but I don't always remember to tell you. Admittedly, this is usually because my life is in danger and too many things are happening for me to think straight, but that's beside the point." Alyssa lowered her feet to the floor, and carefully shuffled over to Abby's bed, and she sat down on the edge of it. "The thing is... I wouldn't have likely survived this year had you not been there for me."

"We're friends. That's what friends do for one another."

"That's true, we are." Alyssa took in a deep breath and let it out slowly. "And about that. I've been avoiding talking about it, but..."

When Alyssa was silent for a few seconds, Abby spoke up. "But we're only friends and nothing more, right?"

"I'm so sorry, Abby." Alyssa took hold of Abby's hand and held it tight. "I don't know if this helps you, but if I was attracted to women, you'd be my first and only choice, and I'd be the luckiest woman in the world."

Abby nodded. "But you're not attracted to women, and I know that."

"You're right, I'm not," Alyssa said softly, "but you are such an important part of my life. You've inspired me, helped me grow, and I love you dearly. I don't know how I'd ever live my life without you. I hope that's enough."

"Yeah, it is."

Alyssa leaned over, put her hands on Abby's shoulders, and gave her a half-hug.

Abby wrapped her arms around Alyssa and held her tight, hoping the moment would last forever. Whether her feelings for Alyssa were true love, a mere crush, or something in between, Abby didn't know. But for now, for this one moment, the world couldn't be any better.

Titles by this author:

Murder Mysteries: The Baneridge Trilogy

The Baneride Murders

A Cruise to Die For

The Witness Who Wasn't There

Dark Comedy (18+)

Love by the Hour

Adventure Thriller

The Future Imperfect

Biography

Through the Woods: Dorothy's Story

Young Adult Trilogy

The Target

The Estate

The Suspect

Manufactured by Amazon.ca
Bolton, ON

32752629R00149